3-17

SAVING
SORROW

A novel by Patty Slack

To Karla —
From the continent that
holds a bit of your heart.
Patty Slack
Luke 6:47-48

Library of Congress Control Number: 2015917361
CreateSpace Independent Publishing Platform, North Charleston, SC

Cover design by Jessica Slack
Cover photo by Johnathan Thomas

For Edwin,

We've gone together, there and back again. You were by my side when we walked at the glacier, when we set up house in Africa, when we had our babies, when I wrote this book.

Thank you. I can't imagine life without you. You make everywhere we go my place to belong.

Chapter 1

CASSIE USED A BIT OF HER PHONE'S precious battery life to snap a selfie. The angles of the face staring back startled her. With no mirror in her rented cement room, she hadn't seen herself in weeks. Years of squinting in the African sun had weathered her. She looked at least as old as her twenty-seven years, if not older. She should be thankful she'd only gained crow's feet and freckles, not the rawhide skin of some of the German expats. One good thing about being a fair-skinned redhead—she wasn't tempted to tan.

She stared at her picture. Forget the face. There was nothing she could do to improve it. But was the dress nice enough? It better be. It was the only presentable thing she had left to wear. She squinched her face up, trying to decide. Maybe the ambassador wouldn't notice what she was wearing.

A girl could hope.

Cassie pulled the heavy wooden door of her room closed and locked it with a chunky padlock. She slung a backpack over her shoulder and started the long slog up to the main road, where she could catch a taxi. Red dust kicked up around her, resettling on her hem, her sandaled feet, her legs.

Her freshly ironed dress wilted in the heat. Not for the first time, she thought about going topless like so many of her friends here. The promise of cooling off was tempting, but she knew shedding her shirt wouldn't actually help in this sultry heat. Not to mention the great potential for sunburn. Red skin and red hair. Wouldn't that be a sight!

"Yovo!" A child, wearing only a loose pair of panties, yelled at her from alongside the road. It was Fabrice, Elli's youngest brother. She always recognized him because he had red hair, too. Only his was a symptom of kwashiorkor, the disease brought on by malnutrition that gave children rusty hair and potbellies. She would pick up a supply of children's vitamins for him before she came back from the capital tomorrow.

Her first few months in Nkuve, she used to smile at every child who chanted the word for "white woman." Now she thought of it as the soundtrack of her life, a record that kept skipping back to the same words over and over, following her wherever she went. She saw these children every day, knew them by name. She had visited their houses, eaten dinner with their parents, helped with their medical bills, and still, the children only called her by the color of her skin. They meant it in fun. They had no idea their playground chant cut her to the soul.

In the taxi van, she squashed between two large women. Their body odor hung in the air. She likely smelled as ripe after her long walk.

One of the women, traveling with three small children, plopped her baby on Cassie's lap without asking. The taxi van started with a lurch.

Cassie smiled at the child and turned it sideways on her lap to keep it from groping her clean dress. She greeted the other passengers.

The baby looked up at her with chocolate eyes. If Crayola could copy that rich color, they'd make a fortune off it. The infant, perhaps three months old, was dressed all in pink with lacy elastic pants.

"Your daughter is beautiful," Cassie said to the mother.

Every woman in the van burst out in laughter.

The mother chuckled and shook her head. "It's a boy!"

Cassie looked again, this time at the baby's ears. No earrings. This frilly bundle of pinkness was a boy. Of course it was.

Whether from the bumpy taxi ride or to show his disgust at her insult, the baby looked Cassie in the eye and spit up on her. He stared at her, startled. Then he started to cry.

Cassie balanced the screaming child with one hand and used the other to hunt for something to sop up the mess. The large woman beside her removed a head scarf and blotted at Cassie's chest, but the waxed fabric only spread the mucusy milk around.

The woman shrugged in apology.

Cassie shrugged back. There was no way to spot clean the dress at this point. She'd have to stop at the dead yovo market in the city to buy a new one—or a gently used one—before the party. She took the scarf and dabbed at the mess herself. She got almost all the spit-up cleaned off when she felt a warm moistness spread across her lap and trickle down her leg.

She was definitely buying a new dress. She would not approach the ambassador of the United States reeking of spit-up and urine.

Jason stepped out of his air-conditioned Land Cruiser, handed his keys to the valet, and entered the air-conditioned residence of the US ambassador. The few feet in between were hotter than a fire walk. He'd read that Nkuve was hot, but he'd never imagined a sauna. It was going to take some time to adjust to the tropics after the brutal winter he'd spent in Lithuania.

Pink Italian tile held the cool air inside a giant foyer. He stepped through the entryway into a soaring living room. Waiters in black suits with white gloves circled the room offering cool drinks in sweating glasses to milling guests. Jason felt sorry for the servers in their formal attire. No one should have to wear a jacket here, or gloves, or sleeves or socks or possibly anything at all. At his last assignment, he learned to wear layers. Here, there were only so many pieces of clothing you could appropriately remove. He expected he'd find that line and sit on it. Either that or spend his short stay here in whatever air-conditioned space he could find.

He accepted a drink from one of the servers. Something about the man's attire and manner made Jason bristle. He didn't like being served by an African. It felt like a step backward into a time that no one should ever want to return to. This was Africa, though. Who else was going to serve drinks?

Looking around the room, he sensed an imbalance between the haves and have-nots. There were no in-betweeners, really. Eventually, he would find his place among the haves, but not today. Today, he was seeking out the American expat version of the have-nots, the Peace Corps Volunteers.

He spotted them across the room, recognized them by their wild African printed pants, their REI sandals, and the way they hovered around the hors d'oeuvres and open bar like condors over a carcass. The outfits might be different here than in northern Europe, but the hunger was the same. He made his way over to them, eager to tap into their notoriously friendly insight on local culture and geography.

A large man blocked his path. The very picture of an ugly American, he had stuffed himself into a business suit too hot for this infernal weather and too tight for his generous neck. His face bloated red above his starched white collar. "Let me get you another drink," he said. He stretched out a hand. "Name's Hal."

"No thanks," Jason said, eyeing the Peace Corps workers but unsure how to break away to reach them. He accepted the handshake. "Jason. Nice to meet you."

Hal's handshake was warm, moist, and flaccid. "How long have you been in country?"

Jason wiped his palm on his pants. "I arrived last night."

"A real newbie, then. What brings you here?" Hal's eyes lit with the possibility of a good conversation, a chance to talk to someone from outside his small, insular expat community, perhaps?

Jason shrugged. "I've always wanted to visit Africa, go on a safari, meet the locals."

"You've come to the wrong place then, son," Hal said with a laugh.

Jason cringed at the paternalistic tone. Great White Father syndrome was nothing unique to Africa, but this fellow seemed to have an exceptionally strong case of it.

"No safaris here, young man. No animals but chickens and goats. If you're wanting to see big game, you're on the wrong side of the continent."

Jason was in exactly the place he needed to be. His prey was not Africa's big five—lions, rhinos, elephants, buffalo, and leopards—but the people of the Bodo Valley. His first step in helping them was to understand them better. And this buffoon was standing in the way of his first step to that end. "Excuse me," he said. "I'm going to get another drink."

"Allow me." Hal waved his hand at one of the waiters and barked out, "Garçon!"

Jason didn't know much French, but enough to know calling a waiter "boy" was quite offensive.

Unfortunately, the waiter responded to the call and approached with his tray of cold drinks. He didn't seem to notice or mind the gaffe.

"Beer?" Hal asked, grabbing for a sweaty mug with meaty hands.

Jason stepped back a couple of steps. "No thanks. I don't drink."

"You will!" Hal let out a loud guffaw. A puzzled look crossed his face. "Wait, didn't you just ask for a drink?"

Jason took another step backward. "You must have heard wrong. I said I need to find the restroom." He turned and looked for a doorway—any doorway—to duck through. He beelined for a set of double glass doors.

Chapter 2

CASSIE EYED THE CROWD. SHE recognized the Peace Corps group by their vibe, not their faces. This was a whole new batch since she'd finished her tour, but they had the same look—relaxed and ragged. She gravitated toward them.

Every flat surface in their vicinity was covered with empty beer bottles and cocktail glasses. Their side of the room smelled like a still.

"Hey," said an impossibly young guy with braided hair. "You new?"

Only recent arrivals braided their hair. The first and last time Cassie had paid to have the tight cornrows plaited across her scalp, she'd had to hack off several inches to even the broken ends. Not to mention the horrible pain of long, thin rows of blistering sunburn. "Nah, not new," she said. She was once, about a million years ago. "Not Peace Corps either."

"Oh, sorry. I just thought, you know . . . your dress."

It wasn't exactly the look she was going for when she picked out the loose-fitting dress in the market on her way here. The image of sacrificing your life for the greater good involved a certain amount of advertising your values through wardrobe choice. She'd given her years as a volunteer, complete with the look, but her idealism had been replaced with the understanding that quick fixes are often no fix at all. To make a real, lasting difference, she'd embedded herself in the culture here, while trying to keep one foot in her own. Her idea of what a young American woman would wear to impress had obviously missed its mark.

"I finished like three years ago," she said.

"That's cool. And you stuck around?"

"I had more to do, I guess." She smiled.

"I hear ya." When he nodded, his braids did a funky little dance like a herd of slinkies bouncing around his face.

Cassie used to love this kind of banter. Now it felt plastic. She was less comfortable at this party than she was in her own small village, where every day brought the tension of life and death into focus. She was ready to get away from the opulence and the facades, back to real life in the real world. But before she went, she wanted to secure the promise of help for some of her favorite people. She excused herself from braid boy. Anyone with *volunteer* in his title would not have the resources she was seeking. From the veranda, she scanned the poolside crowd. It was all bikinis and Speedos, no one in a business frame of mind. She wouldn't be approaching any of them. She kept looking for an easy target, someone with the right mix of money and compassion.

Across the pool, she spied SJ, one of her fellow volunteers back in the day. He was the only one besides her who had stuck around. He taught English in one of the villages south of hers.

He saw her looking at him and waved.

Just as she lifted a hand to acknowledge him, something hit her in the back.

"Ow!" She turned around.

A man stood frozen, framed inside the open French door he had shoved into her.

"Sorry. Excuse me," she said, though she wasn't sure why she was the one apologizing. She was just standing here.

"No, no. My fault." The well-dressed, well-groomed man stuck out his hand. "Jason."

"Cassie." She sized him up. He was a little older than she was, clean, but with the withered look of someone who hadn't acclimated. "You just get here?"

Jason frowned. "Why does everyone keep saying that? Is it so obvious?"

She pointed to his wrists. "Your arms are pale but your hands aren't. You're used to wearing long sleeves."

He laughed. Wow, his teeth were white. "You got me, Sherlock."

Cassie pointed at the door. "Running away from someone?"

Jason's gaze followed her gesture. "No. Well, kinda. That guy was a little pushy, that's all."

Cassie saw several men through the glass door panels, but she knew immediately who he was talking about. "The one in the suit?"

"Yeah."

"He's used to getting his way. That's Ambassador Grimes's husband."

Jason hit his forehead with the heel of his hand. Clearly if he'd known who it was, he wouldn't have run away.

Cassie, who knew exactly who it was, wanted nothing to do with him or his wife, at least not on a social or political level. The reality was, though, they were the whole reason she'd made this trip. She wiped the sweat from her forehead and upper lip. "That's who I've been looking for. Wish me luck."

"Luck," he said. "You're gonna need it."

She'd need more than luck. She was hoping for grace, eloquence, and irresistible charisma. All that and more if she hoped to get any blood out of any diplomatic turnips.

Cassie negotiated her way around Mr. Grimes with some difficulty. She pretended to be part of a conversation about industrial farming, carefully keeping her back to the ambassador's husband as she skirted around the room toward his wife. The ambassador, dressed in a yellow cotton dress, brought the phrase "golden goose" to mind. From the corner of her eye, Cassie saw Mr. Grimes moving closer. She took a half turn toward the bar, then rerouted when she saw that's where Mr. Grimes was heading.

When she finally got to the same side of the room as the ambassador, she realized she wasn't nearly as frightening as her husband. In fact, her yellow dress and short haircut came off with an ease of style that made Cassie want to ask her about how she kept herself looking so cool. Maybe there was some sort of diplomatic training that conditioned ambassadors and their staff—if not their husbands—to resist the urge to perspire. It would come in handy during international negotiations and on hot afternoons like this one.

Cassie waited for the ambassador to finish her conversation with an Nkuvian businessman. She hung back far enough that she wouldn't be seen as intruding, but close enough to hear everything they were saying.

The scars across the man's face indicated he was from the north. She half listened to his plea about the need for clean water and electricity to remote villages. It was an ongoing struggle for the impoverished nation to work toward the infrastructure most of the world considered basic human rights.

She knew he had the best of intentions, but his energy was misdirected. Sometimes what you thought you needed and what you really needed were not the same thing.

Madame Ambassador gave the man her full attention. She nodded and interjected and responded to what the man was saying without making any promises.

Finally, the man grasped the ambassador's hand in both of his and shook it with such enthusiasm he must have thought the United States would be digging wells and stringing power lines to every village in the region by next weekend. He'd heard what he wanted to hear, not what was actually said.

When the man turned away, Cassie saw a fleeting exhaustion wash across the ambassador's face, a small crack in her diplomatic mask. If anything, it set Cassie's mind at ease. At least she'd be talking to a human, not a robot.

Cassie put on her most confident smile and stepped into the ambassador's sphere. This was her chance to find the funds that would make the difference between her friends' children being fed or going hungry. She thought of little Fabrice and how a steady income for his mother would take care of his malnutrition. The amount she needed wasn't even small change to the vast foreign aid budget of the US. She couldn't—wouldn't—go back to Babakondji empty handed. They were counting on her.

She held out her hand. "Madame Ambassador? Cassandra Perth. I am honored to meet you."

The ambassador greeted her with a warm smile.

Cassie couldn't help believing it was genuine.

"Cassandra? What brings you to Nkuve?"

Cassie swallowed. "Development."

"Oh? What agency are you with?"

"None at the moment." Cassie wished she could name a big NGO, but she was a one-man operation for now. "I came with the Peace Corps five years ago . . . Your Excellency."

"Madame Ambassador will do. You didn't go home when your tour was up?"

Cassie shook her head. "This is home."

Ambassador Grimes smiled again. "I admire you for that. Not many people would give up the comforts of American life to call Nkuve home. What project are you working on?"

Cassie chose her words carefully. "I've done several. Chickens. A bakery. But those all depended on me to succeed. I'm launching a microloan project. It will put decisions and ideas in the hands of the small business owners."

The ambassador's smile faded a little. "Have you had any success with your other projects?"

"Circumstances—" Cassie stopped herself. There was no way to communicate all the obstacles she'd hit without sounding like she was making excuses. She rephrased in her head before speaking. "I think it will give the people of my village a way to take their future in their own hands and learn to support themselves with their own ideas."

Cassie felt the change in mood.

Ambassador Grimes's smiled tightened. Her shoulders tensed ever so slightly.

Cassie talked faster to compensate. "Everything is ready to launch. We've got dozens of people lined up with business plans. All we need is the funding to kick things off, and then it will pay for itself. Microloans are going to change their future." She wiped the sweat from her upper lip with the back of her hand.

"Have you considered applying for a grant through one of the programs available to former PCVs? Or through one of the NGOs in the country?"

"A few," Cassie said. "There are probably more I could try, but the amount of paperwork—"

"I'm sorry," the ambassador said. "I don't think I'm the one you need to talk to. There are a lot of other resources available. Call the embassy. They can get you a list."

Cassie blinked. "I—but—"

The ambassador interrupted her. "I'm not authorized to sign a blank check over to every American with an idea. All our funding for these kinds of projects must go through USAID or a recognized NGO. You understand."

Cassie stammered, "In theory, yes. But we're not talking about lifeless statistics. These are real people with real problems and real solutions for their own problems.

They don't exactly have NGOs beating a path to their village. All they need is a little funding."

The ambassador held out a hand to stop her. "You have to look at the big picture. One project in one village doesn't hold the answers. We have to raise the standard of living across the board."

"And how are you doing that?" She'd never seen anyone from the US or any other Western nation offering to help Babakondji.

"Microfinance, to be sure, but we have to attack things on a broader scale. We're finding some trickle-down projects are quite effective."

Trickle down. Cassie cringed. She swallowed her quick comeback and gave herself a breath's worth of time to compose a calm response. "Respectfully, ma'am, I've been in that village five years. Trickle-down economics don't work. I am talking about people who have to scrape their living out of the dirt. Big government projects like improved highways and soccer stadiums don't benefit them. They don't trickle down far enough. Wouldn't you rather drink from a fresh spring than from a leaky faucet?"

"In theory, of course. But focusing on only one solution is myopic."

"Better too close to the problems than too distant."

Ambassador Grimes shook her head. "If we go too grassroots, we lose control on a big scale. You've got to understand the political context we're dealing with. We have to minimize corruption, power grabbing, embezzlement."

"Well, those problems aren't exactly unique to Africa, are they? That's politics," Cassie snapped. Crud. Talk about biting the hand you hoped would feed you. "Present company excepted, of course."

Doh.

"Of course." The ambassador narrowed her eyes. "Most Peace Corps Volunteers figure out during their tenure that they can't actually change the world."

Cassie's cheeks burned. "Not the whole world at once. I just want to change one little corner. I want to build a better life for Elli, for Koffi and Essewa and Enyonam." She wanted to hit something. Either that or burst into tears.

"What about the Central Bodo Project? There is plenty of work in that region for people who are willing to take it. Construction jobs, security, HR. That's where the future lies."

"The dam?" Obviously they were speaking different languages. "That dam is the worst thing that could happen to our region. It's tearing apart the fabric of families. It's displacing people up and down the valley. At least it's not touching our village."

"That dam offers progress, improved infrastructure—"

"—lies and false hope," Cassie interrupted her. "Every benefit from that dam is going straight to the rich."

"Trickle down, my dear. You'll see."

Cassie wasn't trying to keep her voice down anymore. "Oh, I'll see all right. I'll see people shoved out of their homes. Farmers with no land to farm on. Families going hungry—"

"Electricity, jobs, road improvements—"

"—for people without electric lights, skills, or cars! It's the wrong kind of help!"

A light touch on her arm stopped her from saying the rest of what was on her mind. Cassie could still hear the arguments echoing in her mind, but that was the only sound in the room. Everyone at the party had fallen silent to listen to her make a scene. She put her hands up to cover her burning cheeks. She turned to see who had touched her.

The guy who'd run into her outside—was it Jason?—stood behind her, smiling at the ambassador. "Am I interrupting?" he asked. "Excuse us, Madame Ambassador. I have some questions for this young lady about her village." He took Cassie's elbow.

"Good luck, Miss Perth." The ambassador dismissed Cassie and then turned to her next conversation.

Cassie let Jason lead her out the front door. As they crossed the room she felt the icy stares of the other guests. Even her fellow volunteers stared at her like she was an alien life-form.

Jason led her outside and closed the front door on her best chance at funding. She'd have to find another way.

Chapter 3

OUTSIDE, JASON RELEASED HER ELBOW. The sun had dipped below the bougainvillea hedge. Twilight lasted only minutes here on the equator. Soon it would be night.

Cassie stepped toward the door. She wanted to start the conversation over, to take a different tack at the ambassador's heart and budget. She just needed another chance.

"I wouldn't go back in if I were you," Jason said. "Simmer down a little. Ask her again later."

"There's no later," Cassie said. "I need the money now."

"Need or want?" Jason held up a hand. "It's hot out here." He waved the valet over and handed him a key.

The young man went in search of the vehicle.

Jason turned to Cassie. "Get in the car. I'll see what I can do."

"But—"

Jason held up his hand.

Cassie shut up.

"Don't worry," he said. "I'll be right back." He ducked back into the mansion, leaving Cassie to swelter on the marble steps.

Who was this guy? The new guy in town, for sure. So how come he thought he had a better shot with the ambassador than she did?

She waited for the car to pull around, cursing herself for making an idiot of herself and for blowing her chance with the ambassador. She dreaded going home and facing everyone with the disappointing news. She would come up with another idea. She always did. But she hated getting their hopes up only to disappoint them.

The growl of a diesel engine reached her ears before she saw the brand-new Land Cruiser pull in front of the house.

The valet got out and held the door open for her.

Cassie hesitated. She hadn't driven anything in the three years since her last trip to the States. She had *never* driven anything as beautiful as this beast. It was every aid worker's dream vehicle. The good ones would feel guilty about driving one, but they'd drive it anyway. The price of this truck alone could fund a microloan project for a whole cluster of villages. Jason was definitely not an aid worker. He must be in business. She looked at the corners of the car to see if it sported any diplomatic flags. No flags. No special tags. Definitely a businessman.

Cassie scrambled up into the driver's seat. Hot leather stung the backs of her legs through her thin cotton skirt. The air-conditioning blew new car smell across her face like a breath of heaven. Of all the things she missed from home, climate control was at the top of the list.

She tipped her head back against the headrest. How could she have been so stupid? She could be impulsive, sure, but to chew out the ambassador of the United States of America? In front of everyone? She'd never live it down. It was embarrassing and disappointing. Her eyes filled with unbidden tears.

Jason tapped on the passenger's window and mouthed, "Unlock?"

Cassie wiped her eyes with the backs of her hands. She reached across and pulled up the button. She started to open her own door, but Jason jumped in the passenger's side.

"You mind driving?" he asked. "I don't know my way around yet."

"I guess." She didn't mention she didn't drive much, especially in the city. He was an attractive guy, obviously successful, and quite confident. Maybe the ambassador wasn't her last opportunity. She flashed him her winningest smile. "Where to?"

He adjusted the A/C. "Any good restaurants in town?"

She shrugged. "Depends on what you like. Chinese, German, French, Italian."

"Anywhere we can find a good burger? I came straight here from Europe. I've been craving Red Robin."

Cassie laughed. "No American. The only burger place I know of is Lebanese. I'm not sure what kind of meat they use, but it's definitely not beef."

"Your choice, then. Whatever you like best."

She always went for the cheapest option when possible, especially when she was paying her own way. "Is local okay?"

"Sure. It'll give me a taste of that village life you were going on about." He grinned.

Cassie put the vehicle in gear and eased out to the street. The Toyota rumbled beneath her. Fufu was her favorite, and it was on budget. It was also outside, which had its good and bad points. "Are you taking anything for malaria?" she asked.

"Larium. Why? You can't catch malaria from food, can you?"

"Nope, just mosquitoes. You're fine. I know just the place." She gripped the wheel and held her breath as she accelerated into traffic. Daylight was fading fast. No luxury of sidewalks or shoulders in this part of town. Or streetlights. Or pavement. She'd have to trust her headlights and her horn.

The truck's right front wheel dipped into a bottomless pothole. The seat dropped out from under her. She gripped the wheel tighter and turned hard left to avoid the back wheel following.

Jason jabbed his palm to the ceiling to keep his balance.

"Whoops!" Cassie laughed. "I didn't see that one." She leaned forward a little more, tugging against the seat belt to scan for holes and bumps.

"No problem," Jason said, but his voice sounded a little strained.

Ahead, a line of streetlights announced the main road. Cassie advanced slowly. A small goat wandered into the road in front of her, stopping to eat a tasty piece of garbage. Cassie tapped lightly on the brakes. The car lurched to a stop.

"Whoa!" Jason shouted, putting both hands on the dash.

"Sensitive brakes." Cassie felt her face turn red. Thank goodness it was dark enough now that Jason couldn't see how flustered she felt.

"I guess. Maybe I should drive?"

"No, no. I'm fine." She pressed the gas again and lurched toward the streetlight. A red light gave her a chance to survey the road. She needed to go left. When the light turned green, she inched the nose of the vehicle out into the street and eased into a left turn.

"Watch out!" Jason yelled.

"It's okay. I got it." She looked right and saw a taxi van barreling toward them. She couldn't back up and she couldn't go forward. She stomped on the gas and made a hard left just in time. Once she was safely in her lane, she laughed out loud. "You have to be a little aggressive, or you'll never get anywhere."

"If aggressive is the goal, you're doing great."

Cassie smiled. "Thanks." She glanced over at him. He was clutching his shoulder belt in both hands. She swerved around a woman riding her bike. A horn blared to her left. A motor scooter zipped past her window. She pulled the wheel right to give him room. Now which corner did they need to turn at? She knew in the daytime a man with a rickety table sold used stuffed animals there. At night, she guessed that space would be empty. There it was, just an empty lot.

She took a hard right.

Too hard.

Something clanked against the passenger's side fender and screeched all the way to the back of the car.

"Stop!" Jason yelled. "You hit something!"

Cassie slammed on the brakes.

Shoot.

Shoot, shoot, shoot, shoot, shoot.

She fumbled for the door handle and bolted out of the car. By the time she made it around to the other side, Jason was surveying the damage with the light of his cell phone.

"Whatever you hit, you managed to scrape every panel," he said.

Cassie pushed past him to the back of the vehicle. Just behind, a beat-up taxi was parked on the roadside, its driver nowhere to be seen. If she had hit the car, no one would ever know. It looked like it had been in its share of fender benders already. She turned to go back to the Land Cruiser. "No harm done," she said.

"No harm? Did you see my car?"

"Yeah, sorry," she said. She really was, but this was not the time to dwell on it. "We should go."

"Without telling anyone?" He stared at her like she was nuts.

"Yeah. Let's go now." Her foot hit against something that scraped along the ground. She bent to see what it was.

She picked up the chunk of metal and glass. "Looks like the driver's side mirror came off. At least it didn't break." She looked for a place she could set it down.

"Every single panel," Jason said. He rubbed his fingertips along the scuff line that ran front to back on his new car at exactly the height of a car mirror. "I had less than fifty kilometers on it."

"Sorry 'bout that," Cassie said. They were taking too long. She did not want to get caught here with an angry taximan and everyone his yelling would attract. "We have to go. Get in."

Jason walked toward the taxi. "Don't you want to leave a note or something?"

"No."

The taxi driver's window was open . . . or maybe missing.

Cassie tossed the mirror on the seat. "We need to leave. If this guy comes back and sees us here, it'll take all night. I'll leave him enough money to get it fixed." She pulled some CFA out of her purse and tucked the bills under the mirror with a sigh. She could hardly afford to spend money on a stupid mistake like this. She didn't even want to think about what it was going to cost to fix Jason's brand-new Land Cruiser. Any of her depleted personal savings that went for car repairs were funds she couldn't use for microloans. And any chance he might want to fund her was ruined before she even got to pitch to him.

She walked around to the driver's side.

Jason met her there. "What do you think you're doing?"

"We need to go," she said again. She reached for the handle. Her eyes darted back to the taxi.

"I'll drive," he said. He pushed her hand out of the way. "Get in the other side."

Of course he would want to drive. She stood dumb for a minute before she got her feet to move to the passenger side.

"Where are we going?" he asked. "Straight?"

She nodded dumbly.

He threw the car into gear and pulled forward.

She watched the side mirror for the taxi driver. No one came. The money she'd left would cover the repair with enough left over that he wouldn't be disappointed. He'd probably just pocket the cash and toss the mirror in the trunk without fixing it. She glanced over at Jason, who now drove with the intense concentration she had used. Lots of good it did her. "It's up there on the left," she said, pointing to a shack with a tin roof and a string of green Christmas lights hanging outside.

"Rustic," Jason said.

"Tried and true," Cassie replied. When she opened the door, the smell of smoke and palm oil wafted over her. It smelled delicious.

She felt like throwing up.

Chapter 4

THE LITTLE RESTAURANT CASSIE chose hit every one of Jason's senses with an arsenal of Africa. Music boomed through an old-fashioned megaphone speaker tied to a tree with a knot of plastic cord. The melody line crackled above the pulsating bass and drums. There was a definite Caribbean flare to it, only much louder and less subtle. It could have been catchy if it wasn't so overpowering. Under the tree stood an open shack with a little fence railing around it. Green Christmas lights lined the roof and twisted around the corner column of the shack. The smell of smoked fish and spice hung so thick in the air he could taste it.

Jason watched, fascinated by the huge woman stirring a vat of soup with a wooden spoon as long and thick as her arm. Whatever she was cooking, it smelled amazing. His mouth watered at the aroma of meat and heat and smoke and spice. He peered into the pot to see what was for dinner.

A goat's head bobbed to the surface of the bubbling brown liquid, eyeball still attached to the meaty skull by a tendon.

Jason looked away. The glands in the back of his mouth tightened. He tasted salt. He turned to look at Cassie.

The light of the Christmas bulbs washed her in a sickly shade of green. She looked like he felt.

All three tables were occupied. Jason hesitated about where to sit, but the woman with the wooden paddle yelled, "Nanyi! Nanyi!" and waved her spoon toward the table in the corner.

Cassie slid in beside a man with incredibly long fingernails. "She wants you to sit," she shouted at Jason, pointing to the bench across the table from her.

He settled on a narrow bench that bowed beneath his weight. The man next to him greeted him with a toothy smile and went back to gnawing on a chunk of rawhide. Jason swallowed hard. All he wanted was to fill his stomach and to dig a little information out of Cassie, but he wasn't sure he could do either if he had to eat skin.

"What kind of meat do you want?" Cassie asked.

"Not goat." *Please, anything but goat.*

"Bushrat's my favorite. Spicy or extra spicy?"

"Extra spicy. But . . . bushrat? Don't they have chicken?" He never thought goatskin would sound appetizing, but next to bushrat . . .

"Trust me. You don't want the chicken. And you don't want extra spicy. I was kidding. Mild here will burn the hair off your chest."

"Trust you? I've known you for less than an hour, and you've already ticked off a US diplomat and committed a hit-and-run. Poison me and we can call it a night."

She grinned at him. "Fair enough."

A teenage girl brought two Cokes to the table and popped the caps off each of them. Jason reached for his and took a long, cold swallow. You could always count on

Coca-Cola, no matter where you went. He pointed the lip of the bottle at Cassie and asked, "What brings you to Nkuve?"

She laughed. "Remember the Occupy Movement?"

"Yeah."

"My last year of college, on fall break, I joined the occupiers in Founder's Square in Louisville. I pitched my tent and everything. I thought it would be a great way to make a stand against corporate greed and inequity."

He squirmed. He was already several rungs up the corporate ladder when the occupiers set up camp. "And did you?"

"I lasted a week."

"What happened?"

"The demands of the leaders were vague. The movement lacked direction. I figured if I wanted to live without flush toilets and electricity, I could do more good in a third-world country. So I joined the Peace Corps." She took a gulp of soda.

"But you're not Peace Corps now."

She groaned. "No. That would be easier. I'm flying solo, lining up funding for a microloan project. I was hoping the ambassador would have some resources I could tap into, but I blew that shot."

"Now what?"

"Now I look for other options. It's what I do."

The woman at the stew pot shouted something. Yelling seemed to be the normal mode of communication around here.

Cassie yelled something back to her.

The woman lifted the lid off a second pot, releasing a cloud of steam. She reached into the pot with her bare hand, pulled out a blob of white stuff, and plopped it in a shallow bowl. Then she ladled a scoop of red liquid over it from another pot. She fished in the same pot with her spoon until she found a piece of mystery meat. She rejected it, letting it fall back in the stew, and dove again for just the right morsel. When she was satisfied, she plunked the meat over the steaming hot white blob and tipped her chin at Cassie.

Cassie slammed some coins on the table in front of her, then rose and grabbed the bowl. She brought it back to the table and set it between her and Jason.

One bowl. To share.

Jason looked around for some silverware.

"Use your hand," Cassie said.

Now that she mentioned it, Jason noticed everyone else in the place ate with their fingers.

"Really?" Jason said. "It's soup. How do you eat it with your hands?"

"Hand, not hands. Only the right one. And be careful. It's hot." She dipped her fingers into the bowl, pinched a piece off the white stuff, dipped it in the red liquid, and popped it in her mouth. "Piece of cake. Now, you said you wanted to talk about my project?"

"Mm." Jason eyed the blob, but decided to start with something he recognized, a little round, green pepper. "Really about your village. What's it called?"

"Babakondji."

So he had heard her right. "Where is it exactly?"

"North of Dagbo, close to the border."

"What's it like? How many people live there?" Jason popped the pepper in his mouth, chewed it twice, and swallowed.

The burn hit his mouth first. Then his throat.

Then his eyes.

It seared. It took his breath away. He grabbed for his Coke and downed it in one long swig.

His mouth roared with fire. The insides of his ears burned.

He grabbed Cassie's Coke and downed it, too.

"Hold on, hold on," Cassie shouted. "Try this." She dug a piece of white stuff out of the middle of the ball and held it to his mouth.

Jason blinked back tears as he leaned forward and accepted the bite. It was squishy and sticky, like mashed potatoes gone awry. And it didn't do a thing to cool off his tongue. "I need another Coke," he pleaded. He sucked air in through pursed lips, anything to stop the pain.

Cassie shook her head. "Have more fufu. It works like crackers and soaks up the oils. Liquid just spreads them around."

He crammed his hand into the white ball and pulled out a big, sticky mass. He shoved it into his mouth and gummed it. Sweat rolled down his face, stinging his eyes before dripping on the table.

Cassie held out her cell phone and snapped a picture of him.

"What are you doing?" he gasped.

"You'll want to remember this moment. Trust me."

Trust me. There were those words again.

Jason squeezed his eyes shut and breathed. A tear escaped each eye and rolled down his cheeks. "I thought you weren't ordering extra spicy."

Cassie laughed. "I didn't. That was mild."

"That was mild?"

"If you don't pop a whole hot pepper in your mouth."

"I thought it was a sweet pepper."

"You thought wrong." When she grinned, the field of freckles on her nose wrinkled.

"No kidding." The skin around his lips still stung with heat, but his mouth was cooling off enough for him to consider another bite. "What else should I avoid?"

"The little red chilies, but I don't think those are in this sauce." She showed him how to pinch a small piece of fufu, dip it, and put it to his mouth. Somehow she managed to keep her left hand out of the mess and keep everything clean but the tips of her fingers.

Jason had sauce running down his arm and chin. His hand was sticky with the paste-like fufu. He wouldn't be surprised if Cassie snapped another photo of him making another ridiculous memory.

When he looked across at her, she was staring at him. Her eyes were so huge, her red hair stained an off shade of gray in the green light.

He cleared his throat. "You were telling me about your village?"

"Yeah. I love it. The people there are so great. They've really taken me in as one of their own. I just want to give back to them, you know?"

"I think I do," he said. He needed more specific information, though. "How big a town is it?"

"Not big. Maybe three hundred. There are a couple of main families, and everyone is tied into them somehow."

"Is it like a family, or is there a leadership structure?"

"Mmm." Cassie held up a finger for him to wait until she swallowed. "Both. We have a chief and he has his advisers, aka his drinking buddies, depending on the day. He's not the big chief, though. The big chief is down the road in Setope."

"When are you going back?"

"In the morning. I have some errands to do, but I need to go home and regroup about the funding thing. Unless . . ." She looked straight at him. This girl wasn't afraid of anything.

Jason straightened his back and crossed his arms. "You've got a place to stay in town tonight, right?"

She nodded.

"What if I meet you for lunch and drive you home? I'd love to see this village of yours."

"Are you sure? That would be awesome! It would have to be a quick trip if you're coming back here the same day. You don't want to drive outside the city after dark."

Jason didn't even have to think about it. "Absolutely. I didn't come to Nkuve to hang out in a city." He could see the question on her face—*So what did you come to Nkuve for?*—but he wasn't ready to answer that one yet.

Chapter 5

WHEN JASON DROPPED CASSIE off at her friend's apartment, she forced herself to give a polite good-bye and walk slowly to the entry. But as soon as she closed the front door behind her, she broke out in a happy dance. She stomped her feet and pumped her arms. Her hair slipped loose from its holder and whipped back and forth in front of her eyes. She squealed, just a little. It was too soon to count chickens, but she was positive once Jason saw her village and her ideas, he'd write her a big fat check.

Who needed the backing of the US government when you had a handsome stranger with obviously generous funds?

In the morning, she sailed through her banking, picked up a few supplies at an Indian grocery store, and found refuge in an air-conditioned Chinese restaurant before the worst heat of the day hit. Remembering the taxi ride down, she was excited about the prospect of riding all the way home in the fancy Land Cruiser. Just the promise of a full hour of air-conditioning made it worth it.

While she waited for Jason, she nibbled on an order of nem, the tiny egg rolls she loved but didn't normally get because of the expense. Since she was saving the taxi fare, she figured she could treat herself.

The lunch rush here wasn't so much a rush as a trickle. Kutome, with its million-plus inhabitants, was still just a small town in a small country if you frequented the expat hangouts. It was more common than not that she run into someone she knew, so Cassie wasn't surprised when Dawkin, her old Peace Corps supervisor, and his staff came through the door. When he looked her way, she smiled and waved.

His staff went straight to the table the waiter directed them to, but Dawkin walked over to greet her.

"Long time no see," he said.

Cassie motioned for him to take a seat, but he ignored her invite, instead standing above her in a way that made her feel too small. She stood to speak with him eye to eye. "I don't get into town much, not nearly as often as when I was working with you guys. How's the new bunch of volunteers?"

"Bright eyed. Idealistic."

Cassie remembered the feeling. "Like every year's batch, huh?"

"Exactly," Dawkin said. "Listen, I just wanted to say tough luck about your village."

Cassie smiled awkwardly while she searched her brain for anything he might have heard that would cause him to offer condolences. Nothing came to mind. "Why do you say that?"

"Aren't you still in Babakondji?"

Her heart thumped a little faster. "Yes? What have you heard?" She'd been out of the expat loop for so long. Why would the tiny village of Babakondji even be on his radar?

"The dam is almost finished. Your village is on the flooding list."

Oh, that. They were building the dam downstream from Babakondji, but the village was so far away from the river, it wouldn't be flooded. The list had come out months ago, and Babakondji wasn't on it.

She shook her head. "No. It's not on the list. We're up a separate branch of the river. The flooding won't affect us."

Dawkin pulled out his phone and tapped on the screen. "Did you see this? Apparently whoever calculated the flood zone made a mistake. They've added five more villages to the list. There's an article in this morning's paper. Look." He held the phone out to her.

She took it with a trembling hand.

The article, written in French, used stilted language to expose the tragic mistake. Cassie let her eyes gloss over the explanation and land on the names of villages.

There it was. Babakondji.

Her knees buckled. She sank to her chair.

The faces of Esse and Elli, Antoinette, Koffi, Afino and her kids all flashed through her mind. They would lose everything they owned if the flooding took place.

What was she thinking? *She* would lose everything.

He took his phone back. "Tough luck. I know you've poured yourself into your village. What's it been? Three years?"

"Five." Counting her two years in the Peace Corps. It might as well have been a hundred.

"Yeah, tough break." He patted her awkwardly on the shoulder and left her at her seat.

She stared out the window at the beach and the rolling blue ocean beyond. The paper must be wrong. Things got misreported around here all the time. It was sensationalism, a tabloid ploy to stir up a reaction.

But what if it wasn't a mistake? She couldn't just sit here. She had to do something. She stood and stalked to the door.

The head waiter approached her.

"Pardon, madame?"

"Oui?" She felt smothered in here. She had to get outside.

"Vous n'allez pas manger?"

Of course he would think she was leaving without paying her bill, but right now, she didn't care. "I'm just stepping out," she said, pointing at the heavy teak door. "I'm waiting for a friend."

Outside, the noonday heat and the heavy air squeezed her. The bad news took her breath away. Shocking. For a village of people who didn't even have enough to feed their children or send them to school, to lose their homes would be worse than devastating. She wasn't prone to tears, but for the second time in two days, she felt like crying.

She paced up and down the porch, wracking her brain for a solution. She could call the ambassador, the secretary of state, the president. Which president? Nkuve's or America's? She should try them both. She started searching for the number to the White House when it hit her. Elli and Akuvi, Koffi and Kojovi, and all the others . . . they hadn't even heard yet. She had to get to them, had to warn them. Everything else could wait.

How much time did they have?

She realized she didn't know. Had they already started the flooding? Maybe that was why they figured out the calculations were wrong. Surely, though, they would start letting the water flow through and give people time to respond and appeal.

Surely.

She stormed back into the restaurant.

The waiter approached her again, wringing his hands.

"How much for the nem?" she asked him. No time for lunch now. She'd have to make do with the appetizer.

He scurried away to bring her a bill. Far be it from anyone here to just say a price. He'd have to handwrite it on a thin piece of newsprint.

She went to Dawkin's table. He was in a conversation, but this couldn't wait. She interrupted him. "Can I see that article again?"

"Sure thing." He handed her his phone.

She quickly pulled up the article, copied the URL, and sent it to herself. She scanned for details. What was the word for *deadline*?

There it was. April 1. Well, wasn't that ironic.

If she didn't do something, Babakondji would be gone in a month.

"Thanks, Dawk," she said. She turned to find the waiter standing only a foot from her, pinching her bill between his fingers. She didn't even look at it. She handed him more than enough cash to cover it and left before he could fetch her change.

Cassie pushed through the heavy wooden door. Her dress stuck to the backs of her legs. She tugged it free and turned to go.

Jason was mounting the marble steps. It was precisely one o'clock.

Chapter 6

JASON, SOMEHOW, APPEARED AS COOL and put together as if he had just stepped out of an outfitters catalog. He'd make a great advertisement for the high-tech moisture-wicking khaki he wore. She'd always thought the whole fibers of cotton were the best you could do in this climate, but looking at her compared to him was a pretty good argument she might be wrong. Or maybe he'd taken that same no-sweat diplomatic training as the ambassador.

She whooshed by him on the way to his car. "We need to leave," she said. "You don't mind?"

"I don't?" he yelled behind her. She heard his footsteps hurrying to catch up. "I thought we were having lunch."

"TIA. Plans changed."

"TIA?"

He really was a newbie. "This is Africa. Nothing runs on schedule. The only thing you can plan on is that plans will change. Unlock the door?" She tugged on the handle of the passenger's side and waited for him to reach across and unlock it.

The door button went up on its own with a clunk.

She'd forgotten about automatic locks.

Cassie climbed into the car and waited for Jason to make his way around to the driver's side. The car, incredibly, still felt cool. She pulled the seat belt around her and wiggled into place, anxious to get on the road.

Jason climbed in his side of the car. He put the key in the ignition, then turned to her. "TIA doesn't sound like a very good explanation of what's happening to me. I'm hungry. What's so important it means I have to skip lunch?"

"My village is in danger. The idiots on the new hydro project think they're going to flood out my house and the rest of my village. I have to get home. Now."

She could have sworn she saw him flinch.

"They're flooding it today?" he asked.

"Not today. At the end of the month. I just found out about it. My people don't know yet. I have to go and tell them."

Jason turned the car on. "I guess it's good they have you. You know the way?"

"Of course." She pointed for him to turn left onto the Beach Road. They would cross the whole width of the country, keeping the ocean on their right, before turning north to home.

Jason drove with both hands gripping the wheel. His strategy seemed to be to keep straight and steady and let the others—cars, bikes, pedestrians, and moto taxis—maneuver around him. Not a bad strategy for a beginner, though he'd need to learn to adjust to the unexpected if he was going to be a successful driver here. Or successful at life here. Life in Africa was all about flexibility.

"It was in the paper," Cassie said. "The news. We knew about the dam, of course, but our village wasn't on the list. Now all of a sudden it is, but no one bothered to come and tell us about it. Not that anyone would bother with a little village like ours, you know?"

Jason nodded. A thin line of white rimmed his lips. "What's that?" He nodded to the right.

"The port," Cassie said. A couple of huge cargo ships were tied off to a pier. Along the roadside, thousands of vehicles filled makeshift lots. "See all those cars? Castoffs from Europe and Asia. That's what people drive around here, if they can afford to drive. The stuff people from the rest of the world don't want anymore. Same with the clothes. Same with a lot of things. Now some big company comes in and says we need a dam. We have a dam already. Did you know that?"

"Ngorogo."

"Excuse me?"

He shook his head. "Nothing. You're saying there's already a dam in country and they are building another?"

"Yeah."

"Do you know how many dams America has?"

"Lots, but this is no America."

"Seventy-five thousand. And you're right. It's not America, but it seems fair for a country this size to have more than one dam."

"That many?" It was a big number. But none of those dams was going to put her out of her home, which made the one here the most important one. "The one up north generates electricity for Kutome. At least it does if we get enough rain. But it doesn't offer anything to people in the villages. All that power gets sent to the cities and big towns. They're displacing the poorest of the poor to give amenities to the richest of the rich."

A chicken darted in front of the car. Jason gripped the steering wheel harder but didn't swerve.

Cassie turned around and looked for the bird. "She made it! Hell bent on suicide," she said. "Every last one of 'em."

Jason laughed. "So that's where the joke comes from." After a few seconds he said, "Fun fact."

"What's that?"

"The chicken joke dates back to before the Civil War."

"Which Civil War?" Why were they talking about chickens at a time like this?

He looked at her sideways. "The Civil War. In America? Eighteen sixty-something? Abraham Lincoln? Freed the salves? Ever heard of it?"

She was reminded yet again of how recently he'd come, how ethnocentric most Americans tended to be when they landed. She corrected his common mistake. "There's no such thing as *the* Civil War. Nkuve has had three of them."

"Three? Really?"

"The fight for independence in 1968, one for control of the government—also north versus south, by the way—in the eighties, and the nationwide strikes ten years ago, though that one was technically not so much a civil war as a failed coup. The American fight over the emancipation of slaves was just one of dozens if not hundreds of fights that have pitted brother against brother." She looked over at him. She'd said too much, basically called him stupid.

"Touché," he said. "Point taken."

They rode in silence for a while.

Cassie kept her eyes open, watching for her favorite landmarks, the little vignettes that reminded her why she loved it here so much.

They crossed over a narrow bridge. Cassie looked down the river toward a sandbar. She was rewarded with the sight of a fisherman casting his throw net in a circle over the water like a flying spider's web. "Beautiful, isn't it?" Cassie said. "I'll never get tired of it. I wonder if this scene will even exist when the dam is finished."

"Is this the mouth of the Bodo?" Jason asked.

"I think so. Left up here."

"If it's still flowing now, it'll still flow when the dam is done. They release the water to make electricity. It just flattens the river. It doesn't dry it up."

He might be right. Or he might not. Either way, this pretty little scene was a byproduct of decisions made upstream. The people making those decisions probably didn't know or care about anything downstream of the turbines.

They made their way through the little coastal town of Aho and into the rolling hills leading up to Dagbo. The road was clearer here, with only an occasional biker or pedestrian heading toward one town or another. Cassie imagined what it must be like to see these people through Jason's eyes. He'd only been here a couple of days. She wondered if he saw them as props in a *National Geographic* photo essay, as statistics or numbers or poster children. The mass of humanity could easily become faceless.

Even she had to remind herself they were real people. She knew each of them had a life and a story, a family and a farm. Their lives were no more or less valuable than those of her friends and acquaintances back in the States. On a personal level, they were more important. These were the people whose lives intersected with hers every day. These were the people who needed her. Here, she could make a real difference.

They passed a couple of women carrying gigantic bundles of sticks on their heads.

"You can see why I stayed," Cassie said.

"Hmm?"

"I know life is harsh here and it's hard for newcomers to see why I've stayed so long. But look at the people. I mean, *really* look at them. They may be outspoken, stubborn, poor, but they are people. Not numbers. They deserve a chance at a better life."

"You think you can offer them that?"

"Yes. Not to all of them. And not all at once. But one by one I can offer hope." She traced the stitches in the leather door handle. "Just not today. I mean, my whole trip to Kutome was to help people out, but I'm bringing them bad news instead. Take a right. I'm not feeling hope myself, but I will. I'll find it and then I'll share it."

They turned off the tarmac onto the washboard dirt road that led through Dagbo. Red dust kicked up behind the car and settled back in the riffles. It wasn't much of a town, but at least it would stay high and dry. If it was in the floodplain, were there enough voices here that they would be heard? Cassie had to believe there were.

They followed the road north out of town. The closer they got to Babakondji, the more Cassie fidgeted in her seat. She hated to be the one to bring bad news. On the other hand, they deserved to know what was coming. And if she didn't tell them, who would? "Turn at the orange tree with the broken branch."

Jason slammed on the brakes and turned right, but not fast enough. He backed up a little and tried again, this time putting his wheels on the double dirt track. The broken limb brushed against the driver's side. He winced. "I guess that side's going to match the panels you scraped up."

Now it was Cassie's turn to wince. "Did I say I was sorry? 'Cuz I am, you know."

He laughed. "I think what you said was 'Hurry! Let's get out of here.'"

She blushed. "Well, sorry, then. Sorry I was the one to cause it. If it wasn't me, though, it would have been someone else. Everything gets banged up here sooner or later."

"Mine took the sooner route. Or maybe the soonest. I'd had this car all of four hours."

"Yeah. That's pretty fast." She was about to apologize again when a sound reached her from somewhere up ahead, high pitched and mournful. It took Cassie a minute to recognize what was happening. She put a hand on Jason's arm. "Slow down."

"What's that noise? It sounds like wailing."

"It is. Someone died."

Chapter 7

CASSIE COULDN'T BELIEVE IT. A death on top of everything else? This changed her approach. She couldn't barge in and heap bad news on bad. She whispered to Jason, "We need to enter the village with respect."

Primal screams, combined with complex drumming rhythms, coursed through her, the heartbeat of her people.

Jason slowed his car to a crawl. "Is it safe?"

Cassie swallowed. "They're not riled up or dangerous. They're sad. The crying won't last long. Once they've sufficiently honored the dead, they will get to work honoring the day. Just go slowly. When I tell you, stop the car, and we'll walk the rest of the way." She'd never heard the wailing this loud. Someone very important must have died. The chief, perhaps? Or his mother?

A group of women in brightly colored wraps stepped out from behind the tall elephant grass in front of the car. Cassie knew them all. Her best friend Elli stood amongst them, her coffee-colored face shiny with tears and sweat. "Stop," Cassie said.

Jason stepped on the brake. The sudden stop threw Cassie forward.

She jumped out of the car.

Elli shuffled behind the others.

Cassie ran to her and touched her arm.

Elli turned. Her eyes were red.

"Nukae djo?" Cassie asked. "Who died?"

Elli answered. "Miawo kata." *We all did.* Elli fell to her knees. "The dam—"

So they knew. How did they know? Cassie's heart clenched for her friend. She sank down in the dust and clasped Elli's hands in her own. "I know. I came as soon as I could. We'll stop them."

"They are too strong. We are too few." Elli's eyes filled with tears, real tears of sadness and fear, not the crocodile tears that many shed on first hearing bad news.

Cassie wondered if she should be sad as well. Was it wrong that she only felt rising anger? She pulled on her friend's hand. "Come on. Let's go."

She dragged Elli away from the group of mourners with their loud and impotent screams. Elli must believe that joining them was a strong show of support, but it didn't accomplish anything. They had no time for crying. They needed to *do* something. The chief would know what was happening. He was the logical person to see first. "Have you seen the chief? Is he home?"

Elli shook her head. "I do not know. He was there earlier, when the news arrived."

"How did you hear?"

"Someone got the article on their phone. The doctor, I think. He sent it to everyone."

Everyone but Cassie. Even Elli, her best friend, had time to tear her clothes and hair and take a death march through the village, but had not thought to send a text? Did they even remember she was gone? Cassie swallowed the pain of it. "We need to find him."

They wound their way between mud huts. The chief's house, a sturdy rectangle of cement blocks, stood empty save for a pair of guinea hens intent on cleaning up a dusting of cassava flour from the ground.

"He's abandoned us," Elli said.

Cassie shook her head. "No. I can't believe he would do that. He has probably gone to stand up to that stupid company." She dialed the chief's number, but got no answer. "Let's search the village." She didn't know what she expected to do once she found him, but in a fight to save the village, he would be her closest ally. "Where would he have gone?"

"The beer seller's? The witch doctor's? He could be anywhere!" Elli started crying again.

The village wasn't that large. If he was still in town, he'd be easy to locate. Cassie patted Elli's shoulder. "You go look at the beer seller's and the bokono's. I'll check the sodabi place and the market. If you find him, text me and bring him here. I'll do the same. See you soon."

Elli nodded. She wiped her tears and took the path away from the well.

Cassie pretended to go in the opposite direction, but quickly spun back to the privacy of the chief's compound. She pulled her phone out again, tapped in the chief's number, and composed a text.

Where are you?

To her surprise, the faint chime of a cell phone dinged from the corner of the compound behind a couple of palm frond panels.

The panels, built in a small rectangle just large enough for one person to stand inside, were the bathing area of the compound. Why would the chief be taking a shower? At a time like this? With his cell phone?

She typed another quick text, took some quiet steps closer to where she thought she'd heard the phone, and pushed send.

A chime, more muffled this time.

Cassie stepped even closer. The weave of the palm fronds was tight enough she couldn't see anyone behind them. Now close enough to hear the breath of the person behind the panels, she stood perfectly still and quieted her own breaths.

She and whoever stood behind the panel waited in a silent standoff. Cassie slowly filled her lungs and held her breath. All she could hear was the beating of her own heart, the diminishing cries of her fellow villagers, and the occasional squawk of a busy guinea fowl.

And then, suddenly, the buzz of a vibrating phone. Cassie startled. His phone, not hers. She took a couple of long, slow breaths to calm her pounding heart.

"Allo?"

He didn't know she was here.

He spoke very softly. She could only catch half of what he was saying. After a few words in French, he switched to English. She didn't even know he spoke English.

"I thought you were going to call earlier," he whispered.

In the pause, she could hear the muffled voice of the man on the other end of the line. Who would be calling in

English? Was it someone from Ghana or Nigeria? Or England or the States?

"Before the announcement, remember?" He paused and listened, then said, "When is it going to be ready? The village has gone mad." His voice rose with desperation and fear.

Cassie strained to hear the meaning beneath the words.

"If they find out, they will kill me . . ." He cleared his throat. "Soon. And do not forget my family. No, that is not right. I said fifteen. Fifteen. One. Five."

Elli was right. He'd abandoned them.

"Yes, three in the cité. The rest in the smaller houses."

He had struck a deal. The cité would be a neighborhood of Western-style homes surrounding a project like the cement plant in Dagbo or the phosphate mines near Avosa.

Or a new hydroelectric project.

That weasel had done a deal behind the backs of all his people to secure jobs and homes for himself and his family. Fifteen? Only fifteen out of the three hundred?

Cassie clenched her teeth together. Her neck and shoulders tensed. She wanted to explode, but she also wanted to hear. She held her anger tight inside her chest.

"Tomorrow? You are sure? Not tonight? . . . How early? All right, all right. Do not forget."

Behind the panels, everything fell silent. Then a rustling told Cassie the chief was about to emerge.

Shoot.

She looked around for her own place to hide. She had planted herself smack-dab in the middle of the courtyard. Every hiding place was too far away. She could try to run, but one glimpse of her red hair, her pale skin, or her American dress would give her away.

She had no choice but to stand her ground.

Chapter 8

CHIEF GBEZE TOOK TWO STEPS into the open. He stopped in his tracks, frozen by the realization he was not alone. His eyebrows shot up.

His initial shock turned quickly to anger.

"Yovo," he said. He'd called her Cassandra for years. Now he called her "white woman"?

Cassie felt no fear, only contempt. He might hold power over everyone else in town, but she only respected him as far as he respected his people. "I heard," she said. "All of it. The new job, the new house, all of it."

He puffed his chest out and took a bold step toward her. "I do not know what you are talking about."

"On the phone. I heard you making plans for you and your family to get out of town. You've betrayed us."

He laughed. "You heard nothing. You have lost your mind."

"You were speaking English. I'm American. I know what I heard."

"You have been in the sun too long. The heat has made you stupid. I do not speak English. Now let me pass. I have a village to console."

She stomped her foot. What she really wanted to do was have a full-out temper tantrum right in the middle of the courtyard. That was a sure way to keep people from listening, though. They had no patience for childishness.

She knew she would have to word her accusation carefully if she wanted to convince the village the chief had sold them out. And the best place to make it, the place she was likely to find the largest audience, was at the village well, the center of village life, where women and children gathered every morning and evening to draw the water they needed for bathing, cooking, and washing. It was no use trying to talk to this man. She needed to expose him for who he was, and quickly.

She turned and stamped out of Chief Gbeze's compound. As she rounded the corner, she met Elli coming the opposite direction.

"He is not here," Elli said. Her coffee-colored face and neck shone with sweat. "The chief has gone to Kutome. He is going to fight for us."

"No," Cassie said, annoyed that her friend believed the first lie anyone happened to tell her. "He hasn't gone anywhere, not to fight for you or anyone else. He's there." She pointed behind her to the chief's compound.

"Akpe na Mawu," Elli said, thanking God for what was—to Cassie's mind—nothing at all to be thankful for.

Elli took the few steps into the compound and looked for the chief. When she saw him, she ran to him and lowered her head to show respect. "Chief, I am happy to see you. Everyone will be glad to see you remained."

This was ridiculous. They were wasting time. Cassie grabbed Elli's hand and pulled. "Let's go."

Elli pulled against her, her head still bowed to the chief. She wouldn't want to appear rude.

Cassie didn't care how they appeared to the lying scumbag. She had to warn the others. She pulled again and begged Elli to follow her. "Va. Mia dzo."

At Cassie's persistent tugging, Elli finally turned away from Chief Gbeze and followed Cassie.

Cassie started to tell Elli what she had overheard, but the chief followed close behind them and stayed close all the way to the well. Cassie kept turning back to glare at him. He was not afraid of her gaze. She could tell everyone—she *would* tell everyone—but he didn't seem to care.

The well stood in the middle of an open area near the edge of the village. Everyone was here, even the men. The crowd wasn't dense, but thick enough that Cassie had to push her way through. A concrete slab a few feet from the well usually served as a washing rock where the women beat their clothes to get them clean.

Cassie climbed the slab. It gave her several inches on the tallest men in the village. She looked around at the familiar faces looking back at her and steeled herself for the bad news she needed to heap on what they'd already endured today.

One white face stared back at her from the shore of a sea of dark ones.

She'd forgotten about Jason. She took a little comfort in the presence of another American. He might not understand the language here, but he understood her in a way no one else could, simply by virtue of holding the same passport. But she wasn't speaking to him. This news was for everyone else.

She cleared her throat. "Friends. Neighbors. My people. We have heard very bad news today, have we not?"

The news had indeed been terrible. The crowd agreed with an "*Ee*." A woman wailed, but was quickly hushed. The time for mourning was over. The time for action was here.

Cassie held her hands in the air until everyone was silent. She spoke slowly so they could hear past her accent. "I am very sorry. I am sorry to hear that this village will see much water. Babakondji is my home like it is yours."

A murmuring from the crowd made her pause. She began to speak again, finding a rhythm her neighbors could hear and agree with.

"I do not want to lose my home."

They all moaned.

"I do not want to leave this village."

They moaned again, the low sound of agreement.

"I do not want the water to come." She couldn't think of the word for *flood*.

Ooo.

"But there is someone among you who wants all of these things."

On hearing this, a couple of people yelped in surprise.

Cassie pressed on. "He works against you to hurt you."

"Who?" Niko asked for the crowd. "Who is it?" He turned to look at Jason, the stranger among them.

Not Jason. He was just an innocent visitor, though it was obvious why he would be their first guess.

Cassie looked at him to reassure him.

He averted his gaze.

Cassie held her hands up again and waited for everyone to still, but they got louder, more insistent. She raised her voice. "It is Chief Gbeze. He has sold Babakondji down the river."

Everyone just stared at her. No reaction, no surprise.

What had she said? She knew she was loud enough. She reviewed her words. She'd pronounced them all correctly. The idiom must be the problem. They would take her words literally and think she wanted them all to move downriver, which was exactly the opposite of what she wanted.

She rephrased. "He made an arrangement with the power company—I don't know what, but he and his family will be moving to the cité to help build the dam instead of staying here to help fight it."

"Not true!" the chief shouted from outside the circle of her peers. "She does not know what she is talking about."

Everyone turned to look at him.

Cassie raised her voice. "I heard you on the phone. You said it yourself—you are leaving!"

They looked back at her.

"Only to arrange something better for my people."

Again they turned to him.

People looked to Cassie again for a retort. What could she say that would make them see the truth? And what good would the truth do them? "You—you've got to believe me," she said, lamely.

"Ha!" the chief blurted. "Why should they? Who are you? Just a stranger who comes in and tries to tell us how to live."

"I'm not a stranger." She had given them five years of her life, five good years, and the promise of many more. "I speak your language. I eat your food. I wear your clothing." She looked down at her new dress—the one she'd been so pleased to find in the Kutome market—and her Keens. She realized it wasn't true. She wore their clothing when it suited her, but she was more comfortable in pieces from the States. She often ate their food, but she was just as likely to take their ingredients and make a taco, a sandwich, or an omelet. But she did belong here. This was home more than Arkansas would ever be again. "I am trying to help you. To help us. We have to work together to stop them from taking everything we own. And we have to stop him." She pointed at the chief again.

He replied with a sneer.

"I for one am going to fight this decision! Who's with me?" she asked. When she didn't get any quick responses, she kept talking. "It's not fair what they've done to us. They make a mistake and we have to pay? They haven't even offered us anything in return."

"They will." Jason's voice came loud and clear, and in English, from where he stood under the old gourd tree.

She stopped. How did he know what was going on? He didn't speak Ewé. She scanned the faces around Jason for someone who spoke English. It must be the schoolteacher interpreting.

"What did you say?" Cassie asked, directing her question over everyone's heads, though she knew exactly what he had said.

"I said they will be compensated. They just got the news today. Give them time."

"Time? We don't have time. They're telling us this valley won't even exist next month. Can you imagine it? The water will be above our heads a hundred feet. All of this, our houses, our farms, our memories, will be buried alive, never to be seen again."

"You're being a little melodramatic, don't you think?" Jason waved her toward him. "Get down off your pedestal. They're not listening to you anyway."

He had that much right. Everyone was talking to someone else. No one was looking at her or watching her, except Elli, who had a look of anguish on behalf of her friend. Cassie, deflated, took a step down. No one even noticed. She wasn't being melodramatic, only realistic. They needed her to help them see the big picture of what was happening. She was the only one who could make these people see that they had the right to fight for their homes and their livelihoods.

These people.

She shook the phrase out of her head. It was much more personal than that.

Her people.

Chapter 9

YOU HAD TO ADMIRE HER PLUCK. Jason gave her that much. One woman standing up to a whole village of angry people who were about to lose their homes. She knew she was in the right—at least in her view—and she was ready to fight for what she believed. No one else in the whole town seemed to have that kind of spirit.

Which worked out well for him.

It meant he'd be able to relocate everyone with very little trouble.

He'd already worked out the deal with the chief and his family, a very fair deal that gave the men and single women respectable jobs at the new hydro plant. The chief would act as liaison between the company and his people. The rest would work as housekeepers, gardeners, and night watchmen for the executives who would stay on-site until the dam had been functioning for at least a year.

With the chief's family taken care of—fifteen adults and their spouses and children—that left just fewer than three hundred in Babakondji. Add the other four villages, all of similar size or smaller, and it was right around a thousand people being relocated. He'd never worked with so few people before, but with this short a timeline, it was best if he had feet on the ground to keep things moving. So far, things were going well, but tensions could get high.

Progress wasn't possible without change. And he found many people, no matter where they lived, were averse to change.

That's where Cassie came in. Once she settled down, she'd be a great ally for him in helping people sign up for new housing. He'd been lucky to find her. Just by being a resident of Babakondji, she made his job easier. Often on projects like this, he had to wade through all the prejudices about Americans. She'd already done that groundwork for him. Here, he could walk through town as Cassie's guest, and no one would think it strange. These people were used to—what was the word?—yovos?

Things were unfolding so quickly here, he hadn't decided how to talk to Cassie. If he told her what he was doing here, she would shut him out in a second. Better to let her warm up to him first, get to know what drove her to stay here, and then find a way to use those motivators to help her help him.

She'd make a better ally than an enemy. With the right nudges, he could help her understand the benefits he was offering her community. Maybe he could even change her mind.

Ha! He might have only known her for twenty-four hours, but he didn't think changing her mind was likely. He couldn't tell her now, though, not when she was so riled up.

He watched her make her way over to him. As she got closer, her bravado faded and her insecurity shone through her eyes.

"Big day for you," he said.

"You got that right."

"I can leave if you want."

She shook her head. "I—no. You can stay. I'm just—I'm reeling. What am I gonna do? I dragged you out here to show you my projects, and now I don't even know if I'm going to have a house, much less people to work with or chickens to coop. I—I think I need to sit down."

Her face, even in the burning sun, was whitewashed with—what? Exhaustion? Defeat? Nausea?

"Let's get you something to drink," he said. He reached for her wrist to lead her to a place she could sit, but she shook him off.

"Not here," she said. "I've got some Cokes at home." She wobbled away, dragging her feet through the orange dust.

"Are you okay?" he called after her.

When she didn't answer, he jogged up behind her and followed a half step behind her in case she decided to faint.

She stumbled.

"Are you okay?" he said again. He reached out a hand to steady her. As soon as he touched her elbow, he pulled away again.

She turned and gave him a little half smile of gratitude. But was she thanking him for helping or for pulling back quickly? He was usually good at judging people, but she had his head in a muddle.

He followed her between the houses to a long cement building with four doors.

"This is it," Cassie said. "Home sweet home."

It wasn't a fancy place by any means, just a row house with a wavy asbestos tile roof. His bike shed back home was nicer. Compared to the places surrounding it, though, this was Buckingham Palace. At least it had solid cement walls instead of mud ones. And it had a huge plastic water tank up top, which meant Cassie had at least some form of running water.

Interesting.

She unlocked her front door and pushed it open.

Jason stepped in behind her. The sun had baked its way inside. She lived in a brick oven. Jason mopped his forehead with his sleeve.

This single room wasn't nearly as spacious as it appeared from outside. She must share the building with others. She had a lumpy mattress on a low wooden frame, stuffed with corn husks by the looks of it. A couple of chairs and a low table made up the living area. An electric fan stood in the corner, covered in dust. He was sure there was no electricity to the village. A tiny blue sink in the corner was her only other nod to modern convenience, that and the small red cooler beneath it.

Cassie sank down onto one of the two chairs, a wooden armchair with no cushions. Droplets of sweat beaded on her forehead. Her freckles stood out against her pale cheeks.

"Let me get you some water," he said. He reached for a cup beside the sink and went to fill it.

She held up a hand. "Nuh-uh. That water's not safe. I've got some Cokes in the cooler."

He opened the old red Igloo. He saw orange soda and Sprite, but no Coca-Cola. "There's no Coke. Is Fanta okay?"

She looked at him funny. "Any kind of Coke is fine."

When he grabbed the bottle of orange pop, he was surprised to find it as warm as the day. Calling that box a cooler was wishful thinking. "Where's your bottle opener?"

She stretched out her hand, and he gave her the bottle.

She tilted the cap end against the edge of her coffee table and gave the bottle a pop with the heel of her hand. The cap came off, spun for a second, and settled in the middle of the table.

"Nice trick."

She took a long swig. Holding the bottle close, she settled back in her chair with a sigh. She closed her eyes and sat very still, still enough he could count the freckles on her eyelids. Color returned to her cheeks. "Want some?" she asked, tipping the pop toward him.

"Uh, no thanks." He wasn't sure if she was offering a drink from her own or telling him to help himself. Either way, he'd grab a cold drink on his way back to the city. "You have running water."

"For the last couple of years. I used to go to the well. I was using all my energy just living and didn't have any left for my work."

"Where does the water come from?"

"A truck refills the tank once a month. It's gravity fed. Solar heated, too, but just because the tank gets so hot. Nothing fancy. It's less authentic, I know, but it was a sacrifice I had to make if I wanted to accomplish anything."

Looking around the room, he could think of a lot of things he would consider a sacrifice. But she chose the one amenity and considered it a compromise of her ideals.

"And the fan? You have electricity?" He'd been told none of these villages was on the grid. When they relocated the village, the promise of steady power was one of the perks he was able to offer. If everyone already had power, they wouldn't be impressed by the promise.

"Yes, no. Well, sort of. We make electricity. That's one of my projects. I've got a car battery for people to charge their cell phones. Sometimes I use it to run the fan at night. I'd love to start that as a business for someone. I also run the light and the fan off solar sometimes."

"So there's no power to the village?"

"Not from outside, but we manage even without the huge power conglomerates." She made a face when she said the last word that told him exactly what she thought of him and his type, not that she knew he was one of them.

He noticed a pile of grass on the floor next to her chair. "What's that? Your chicken nest?"

She laughed. "Not quite. It's a basket-weaving project I'm working on. I'm hoping to find stores in America that would be willing to sell them for us."

To him, it looked like a pile of hay dyed all colors of brown. Some of it had been twisted into knots, but he didn't see anything that resembled baskets. Must be a really new project.

"The chickens are out back. Want to see them?"

"Sure," Jason said.

Cassie led him behind the house. "Here's my girls. I'm up to a dozen hens and their chicks. Thirty-two in all."

He couldn't see anything special about the scrawny birds. A couple of them were mostly bald, though they didn't seem to notice or mind. "You don't keep them penned?"

"Not all the time, but look at this!" She led him to a garden area and pointed to an obviously hand-built box made of random-sized lumber and slightly crumpled chicken wire. "Ta-da!"

Obviously, she expected him to be impressed. "So, tell me about it," he said.

"It's a chicken tractor."

"Chickens pull a tractor?" He pictured a team of six white hens pulling the heavy box behind them.

"Not pull. Live in. It helps me keep them in one area of the garden. They pick out the pests and slugs in one area while they fertilize it. And it keeps them out of the rest of the field. They're terrible about eating baby plants, you know."

"Uh, of course they are," he said. What he knew or cared about plants or chickens wouldn't fill a business card. "Do people even have gardens around here? It seems like the houses are too close together. All I've seen growing in town is dirt."

She laughed. "No, they do. I mean, that's a problem because their farms are outside the village. It was a good idea"—she pointed to the chicken tractor—"but people don't want to keep their chickens far away from home. It's too hard to keep an eye on them when you don't live on your farm. Back to the drawing board, as they say."

"They do say that." Whatever guilt he might have been carrying because he was shutting down her project dissipated. There was no project here, just an unending stream of failed ideas and vain attempts to improve the lives of a handful of people in a remote corner of the world. If anyone was going to make a lasting difference in these people's lives, it was him. At least he had the means and the system to move them off this sunbaked land and compensate them for their loss, such as it was.

Even Cassie, with all her high ideals and Pollyanna look into the future, could easily set up something at least this good, probably better, in the new location, wherever that would be.

Her laugh jarred him. She was obviously not tracking his train of thought.

"You know, these chickens would be better off if we just let them roam free. What with the dam and all. At least they could get themselves out of the way of the wall of water that's fixin' to come swooshing through here."

Jason smiled at the image. There would be no wall of water, of course, just the slow rise of the river like the tide coming gently in. Only this tide would never go back out.

"Well, anyway, that's my projects," Cassie said. "You might be the last one to ever see them." She stopped talking and screwed up her face. "You see there, I'm just like them. With that attitude, I might as well pack up and leave now. But I'm not going to do that."

"You're not?" He could only wish.

"Of course not. I just need a little time."

"For what?"

"To figure out a way to stop the dam. At least I can delay it, right? I just need to come up with the right idea. I'm full of ideas."

"I can see that." If she weren't so dead set against him, he might find her earnestness comical. She was scrappy, though, and determined. In another part of the world, she'd have a fighting chance. All she'd need to do was slap a lawsuit on it, protesting the demise of the silvery minnow or the giant catfish or some other such slippery creature. Any environmental concerns could stop all kinds of progress in most of the developed world. But here—though he'd only been here a couple of days, he had a good sense of it—here a threatened lawsuit would be no contest against a system of bribes and corruption that kept the gears of progress moving and the palms of those in power well greased.

"You can try," he said, knowing she had little hope of succeeding. Still, in the course of the afternoon, she'd managed to stumble across some important information about the chief's participation in the village's demise. If she could figure that out, what else was she apt to learn? His job, or an important part of it, was to keep her from learning it, especially if it was something she could use against the ETN.

She looked into the distance. "You need to leave."

"Pardon?" Did he say something out loud, or was she just that intuitive?

She pointed at the sky. "It's after four. You'd better go."

"I'm happy to look at more projects if you want. I'm not in a hurry."

"You should be. You do not want to be driving here after dark. It's one of the most important rules."

"It is?"

"No streetlights, no shoulders on the road. Dark people in dark clothes. People who have no idea how much damage a speeding car can do. Promise you won't drive after dark?"

He held up two fingers. "On my honor."

She was overreacting. He'd leave, but he saw no reason to keep the don't-drive-in-the-dark-ever rule. That's what headlights were for.

Chapter 10

CASSIE SAT ALONE IN HER ROOM that night. The hum of the electric fan droned a steady note. She usually loved being in the village after dark, after all the children, cars, and motos in Babakondji had been tucked in for the night.

Often, on nights like this, she would listen to the talking drums passing messages from hillside to hillside like a primitive Facebook feed, stories of sickness and death, celebrations and birth.

Tonight the drums were silent.

The coconut palm behind her house shed a frond with a crack and a whoosh! She'd never hear a sound like that back in Arkansas. A sausage bug thrashed clumsily against the window screen. The long, thin insect was harmless, and she left it to its directionless escape attempt. A chorus of camel crickets chirped out complaints about the heat that would last most of the night. This was Africa at its purest.

It must be nearly midnight, but she couldn't get settled. How could anyone sleep on a night like this? Bad news piled on bad news for her village. Just thinking about it, she wanted to cry. Crying wouldn't help, though. She needed to *do* something.

She went outside to stretch her legs. The branches of a giant mango tree obscured the western sky with the interlacing fingers of its leaves. Overhead, the heavens shone bright with a map of stars far more detailed than the one back home.

The Southern Cross hovered like a kite. The sticks that held the kite out tight gave these stars their name. On the other side of the sky, low on the horizon, was the Big Dipper. These stars tied her to the sky of her youth. It was corny, but knowing she could see the same stars as her family back home reminded her that she still lived on the same planet. Sometimes it didn't feel like it.

An owl hooted somewhere beyond the confines of the village, a haunting cry that echoed Cassie's mood. It had taken her years of learning language, of asking inane questions, of gathering answers and practicing responses, to worm her way into the heart of this village. Without Babakondji, who would she be? Where would she go?

She wouldn't. That was all there was to it. She wouldn't move. She belonged here, and so did her neighbors. Why should the guy with the biggest wallet get to dictate the fate of the poor? Why should the power company be allowed to move a village? Why not the other way around?

A car motor grumbled to life nearby.

No one in the village ever traveled at night unless there was an emergency.

She grabbed her avo and wrapped the large rectangular cloth around herself. If someone was sick, maybe she could help. Outside her door, she slipped her feet into her well-worn flip-flops.

The sound of the motor came from the chief's side of town.

She started toward it, but the car was on the move. She changed course. Before she could see who it was, the car reached the road on the edge of the village. Its low grumble faded into the distance.

Cassie hoped whoever it was would be all right. The nearest hospital, the one in Dagbo, was adequate for common illnesses like malaria, but for anything more serious, they would have to go at least another half hour if not all the way to Kutome.

At least they had a car to take them. She turned toward home.

Behind her, a moto growled to life, then settled to a whine. Another moto joined in, again from the chief's side of town.

It hit her. Of course! They weren't sick. They were leaving. It was an exodus! And in the dark of night.

The weasel!

She listened for more vehicles. One car and two motos wouldn't hold the chief and his whole family, much less their stuff. Cassie turned back around and stomped toward Gbeze's house. Unless he was a coward, he would still be there. Before today, she never would have considered he might be. But after what she'd seen in him this afternoon, hiding in the shower, plotting against the town that placed its trust in him, *coward* was mild compared to all the other names she wanted to call him.

She found a handful of adults sitting quietly around the cold fire. The little metal stove they used for cooking was gone. In fact, most of the objects that had been in the courtyard earlier today were gone. The water jugs, the palm frond broom, even the clothesline were missing. It was nothing like the scene she'd expected to find, the family huddled against the walls of their houses and compound, trembling in fear at the thought of being caught like the von Trapp family hiding from the Nazis.

Cassie looked for Chief Gbeze, but in the dark, she could only see people's outlines, not their features.

"Is the chief at home?" she asked. Her voice, the first she'd heard since Jason left hours ago, echoed loud in her ears. The harsh tones of the Ewé language sounded suddenly foreign coming from her mouth.

"He is not here." It was the hollow voice of one of the chief's wives, the older, fatter one. Cassie didn't know her name. Everyone just called her Mama.

"Where is he?"

Mama shrugged.

"When will he be back? I need to speak with him. It's important."

She shrugged again.

Cassie swallowed her anger with difficulty. It wasn't Mama's fault that her husband was a slimeball. "Is he coming back?"

Mama turned away from Cassie.

Moving on, Cassie asked the younger wife, "Do you know if he'll be back?"

She answered with a low "Ooo." She didn't know. Or she wasn't saying. The infant tied to her back with an avo started to cry. The mother rocked side to side until her baby relaxed.

Everyone fell silent. No one offered her a seat.

She squirmed. She wasn't welcome here. She took a step backward.

No one tried to stop her.

She took another step back, wishing she'd never come in the first place. She should have stayed home like everyone else. She couldn't be the only one who had heard the cars, but she was the only one who had come.

She stepped back one more time before she turned and fled. Even in the dark, she didn't want them to see her tears.

Cassie thought morning would never come. The stupid sausage bug still beat at the window. She caught him and let him out the door. When she did, a dozen or more flying termites let themselves in. She sat in her cushionless chair and counted the seconds until morning. She needed to tell someone—anyone—what the chief and his family had done. By the time she finally heard the brush of her neighbor's broom against the courtyard dust, she was as wound up as a stretched rubber band. She shot out of the house like a marble from a slingshot.

"He's gone!" she shouted, aware that her voice was too loud for the predawn hour.

Antoinette stopped sweeping. She looked up from her bent position. Her breasts hung free. "Who?"

"Chief Gbeze. He is gone. Him and his whole family."

"And?"

"And that proves it. He's left us here to sort out how to save the village on our own." Somehow, the subtleties of a second language escaped in moments of high emotion. "I saw them leaving. He took the whole family."

Antoinette straightened. She raised one eyebrow. "Maybe they just went on a trip."

"In the middle of the night? With everything they own?"

"Evo. Evo." Antoinette used the words for *It is finished* as if she was shushing a crying child.

"No, it's not." Cassie grabbed her hand. "Come on. I'll show you." If she could only see, she would understand.

Antoinette dropped her broom and followed reluctantly after Cassie.

When they reached the chief's house, the rising sun washed the red mud walls in pink. The courtyard stood empty, like Cassie knew it would. The family had even taken the benches. A couple of plastic chairs lay upended in the corner of the yard, and the chief's favorite chair, a giant ebony throne, remained in its place. The wooden door to Chief Gbeze's house, which would normally be locked against theft, stood open.

Antoinette walked to it and peered inside.

"Agoh!" she called, clapping her hands. "Is anyone home?"

"Nobody is here," Cassie said. "I told you. They left."

Antoinette stepped into the house. She was inside for a minute before coming back out. She furrowed her brows. "Is it true?" she muttered.

She paced the edges of the compound, stopping here to pick up a little dirt and rub it between her fingers, there to poke at a piece of discarded cloth with her toe. At the far corner of the yard, she let out a yelp.

"What is it?" Cassie stepped toward her landlady.

"They are gone!"

Of course they were gone. Wasn't that what she'd been trying to say?

Antoinette pointed at the ground, as empty as the rest of the courtyard.

There was nothing there. "What is it?"

"The family idol is gone. And the thunder rods." She hurried over beside the house and looked at the ground. "And the legba. All the family gods are gone. They have left forever." When she looked up, her eyes shone with fear.

"That's what I've been saying." Wasn't that what she'd been saying?

"Who will help us now?"

"We will." At least Antoinette was on the same page as her now. If more people grasped what was happening, she wouldn't have to fight alone. "We have to do it ourselves."

"But how?"

"We'll have to work together. Can you show the others what you've seen here? I've tried to warn them, but they can't hear it from me." In this situation, it would better if she wasn't even here. She could start rallying outside resources if Antoinette could spread the word in town.

"Show them what?" Antoinette asked.

"The jugs are gone, the benches, the clothing—"

"The idols. I will show them the empty corner, and they will know."

Cassie nodded. Now they were getting somewhere. "You do that. Can you handle it on your own?" At this point she would be more useful bringing in outside resources than doing a repeat of yesterday's spectacle.

"Yes." Antoinette adjusted her wrap to cover her chest. "Where will you be?"

"I need to get a bigger understanding of what is happening. I can make some calls. We'll need accurate information to be able to put together a plan."

"You will come back?" The concern in Antoinette's eyes confirmed what Cassie already knew—they needed her.

"Of course I will. Give me an hour."

Antoinette would gather and rally the village. Cassie would gather information and rally support from outside.

Cassie left Antoinette to spread the news. She ran home to unplug her cell phone from its car battery charging station. Full life for now. Hopefully the battery would last long enough to call everyone she needed to. She'd start with the newspaper in the hopes they had more details than they had shared in print. Or that they'd collected new information since yesterday. At the least, they could point her in the direction of their source, whether it was the power company or the engineering firm or some third party that had screwed things up and wouldn't admit it.

Calling the paper wasn't as easy as it sounded. Internet was spotty at best down in this valley. She'd have to climb higher to get a clear shot at a cell tower. Not for the first time, she wished she hadn't loaned out her bicycle to the friend who—through no fault of his own, if she was supposed to believe him—ran it straight into a tree. Normally, the easy pace of life suited her. But when you need to get something done in a hurry . . . well, *hurry* didn't translate into life here.

Cassie smeared sunscreen on her bare arms, the tips of her ears, and her cheeks and nose. The sun wasn't high, but it was already getting hot. Twenty minutes to the top of the hill, fifteen minutes back, and some time for asking questions in between equaled a lot longer than her skin could take. She tossed the sunscreen in her bag, just in case, and slung the bag over her shoulder.

She'd walked this road many, many times. She remembered the first time, but never considered that there might someday, not by choice, be a last time. How high would the water reach? Would people one day fish from a shoreline above her head? Would the whole valley become a lake? It might be barely a dot on the map to most people, but in the lives of her friends and neighbors, it meant the end of the world. For their sakes, she climbed faster. Fabrice, Elli's youngest brother, ran after her. "Yovo!" he called.

She stopped for him to catch up. "You want to climb with me?" she asked.

He nodded and put both arms up for her to carry him.

She grasped him by the armpit and swung him onto her back. He snuggled against her. He smelled of dust and smoke.

When she caught sight of the cell tower on the next hill, Cassie put Fabrice down and shooed him home. She turned on her phone. She searched the Internet for the *Ebésé*, the paper that had broken yesterday's news. She'd often been amused by the name of the tabloid. Pronounced almost like "A, B, C," the name of the rag actually meant "spicy." It had a reputation for shock, if not for accuracy. Once she found their number, she listened to the phone ring on the other end. Once. Twice. Three times. Maybe it was too early to call. Maybe they weren't the ones she needed to talk to. What was she going to say anyway? Just as she was about to hang up and rethink her approach, a woman answered the phone.

"Allo?"

Cassie paused. French or Ewé? She chose French. "Hello. I need to speak with someone about an article that ran a couple of days ago. It was about the dam being built on the Bodo."

"Oui. Who wrote the article?"

"Hold on." Cassie checked her e-mail to pull up the article and find the byline. "Pierre Asigbe. Is he in?"

"Not today. He's in the field covering another story. I could have him call you back if you'd like?"

"Sure. About how long will that take?"

"I will try right away, but it could take some time. It depends on if I can reach him."

Cassie shook her head. She'd have to stay on top of the hill until he called. If it took him long, she'd fry. "D'accord. But please ask him to return the call right away." What choice did she have? After hanging up, she looked around for a tree to sit under. It might be only eight in the morning, but the phrase *mad dogs and Englishmen* still came to mind. Nobody in their right mind would choose to sit in the direct tropical sun even early in the morning.

She chose a spindly eucalyptus tree for shelter. Its shade fell in thready curtains that shifted in the light breeze. Better'n nothing. She leaned against its trunk and looked out over the landscape. She was facing the ocean, though it was much too far away to see. She turned to where the river must be, trying to locate where they were building the dam, but she couldn't see it either. Down in her own valley, she couldn't even see the creek. It ran dry this time of year, but the bed it had carved out for itself would soon be used to hold potential energy for people beyond the distant hills.

Her blood boiled, thinking about the haves taking from the have-nots.

It wasn't just her blood that was heating up. Today was sure to be a scorcher. Sweat stood on her forehead, neck, and back. She leaned over and used the hem of her wrap to dab at her mustache of perspiration. She pressed the front of her shirt against her chest. As soon as her cotton shirt absorbed the moisture, new sweat sprang up. It was a losing battle.

Her phone jangled out the chorus to Toto's "Africa." Cliché, yes, but she liked it. She answered, already a little out of breath from nerves.

"Allo?"

It was a man. "Is this Cass-ahn-drah?" He hardened the sound of her name.

"Speaking."

"This is Pierre. I'm told you had a question about one of my articles?"

"Yes. The one about the dam. Thank you for calling back so quickly." She stood and started pacing.

"Which one? I have written many over the months."

"The one about the villages that are fixin' to be flooded. Yesterday's." Was it really only yesterday? Unreal. "I was wondering . . . where did you hear this news? Is it true that they will be flooding more villages?"

"It is true."

"I need to stop the project."

Pierre laughed in her ear. "Stop the project? It is much too late. All the fighting took place months, years ago. The dam is nearly finished. They have stopped the water. They have set the date for the dedication ceremony. The president will be there."

"It's just—I live in one of those villages. We need time to fight. They've taken away our biggest defense by denying us the time to prepare our resources."

"Cass-ahn-drah. What kind of name is that?"

"Um, Greek, I think." Cassandra was the daughter of the king of Troy.

"You are from Greece?"

"What? No. I'm American."

He whistled. "Ah."

Ah? What did that mean? "Is that a problem?"

"No, no. Just, it's interesting. Five villages just found out they are going to be flooded, but it is an American who calls me."

She'd had the same thought. Why did she have to be the one? "What would you do? If it was you, would you just take it, or would you do something?"

"My weapon is my pen . . . well, actually, my keyboard."

"You're suggesting I use a keyboard?"

"Not suggesting, merely answering your question. *I* would fight like I always do, with words."

"What about me? I'm not a writer. Even if I wrote something, who would read it? Will you use your keyboard to fight for us?"

"Listen. Cassandra? I do not even know you. I am reporting what happens. It is not my job to make things happen, just to tell when they do."

"So you won't help us?"

"You figure out what to do, and I will write about it, if it is newsworthy. That is the best I can do."

"But if you write something, people will notice."

"Not if it is not interesting. Make it interesting. Make me need your story. Then we can talk."

That was it? She needed more from him. "Wait! Don't hang up! What about your source?" At least if she could follow up on the source, she'd know who to call next.

"What about him?"

Oh, so it was a man. "Can you put me in touch with him?"

"I cannot give you a source name, normally. But, as I said in the article, the statement came officially from IMAN. They are doing the PR cleanup and negotiations on this situation."

In the article—he'd given a source in the article, and she hadn't even seen it. What else had she missed? She muttered, "Okay, thanks," and hung up. She pulled up the article again and, sitting under the eucalyptus tree, read it in its entirety.

(Kutome) – Only weeks from the dedication of the Central Bodo Hydroelectric Project, Enérgie Totale d'Nkuve (ETN) has released an amended version of its environmental impact study, which redraws the line of villages needing evacuation to include an additional five villages.

The newly impacted area encompasses a tributary of the Bodo River. The villages added to the list of those being evacuated are Kisikondji, Batokope, Babakondji, Sesena, and Asengbe.

A federal court injunction issued Tuesday in Kutome ordered the ETN to provide adequate replacement housing and relocation expenses to the more than 8,000 residents who will be forced to leave their home by the rising waters of the Bodo River. This number includes previously impacted villages, as well as those recently alerted.

The dam is part of a trio of hydro projects being built in Nkuve. The first dam, the Northern Bodo Hydroelectric Project, went online near Ngorogo in 2011 and provides 53 megawatts of electricity to residents of Nkuve and its neighboring countries.

Emanuel Gbedegbe, a representative for the IMAN Group, blames WAEC NKUVE for its inaccurate depiction of the impact area. WAEC was closed due to noncompliance with government regulations in 2013, but the ETN failed to verify the firm's reports and impact boundaries at the time.

The Central Bodo Dam is near completion. Citizens within the boundaries of the original flood zone have already been contacted about a relocation package, or have signed a waiver releasing rights to property in exchange for monetary compensation. Relocation of residents of the remaining five villages will be expected to comply with evacuation orders by March 20, and complete evacuation will take place by April 1.

When she'd read it yesterday, she had only read down as far as the list of towns that were being added to those that would be flooded. Now she carefully read all the way to the end, taking in every word. She learned the name of the PR firm, the date of the dedication ceremony, and the relocation date. In the last paragraph, she learned the most important piece of all. Land and home owners in the villages listed would be either relocated or compensated for their loss. The article did not detail the terms of those packages.

Everyone in Babakondji owned their home. Everyone had a small farm plot outside of town, but she owned neither land nor home. She was a renter, a squatter of sorts, with no permanent ties to the place of her heart.

Everyone would be compensated.

Everyone but her.

Chapter 11

CASSIE PACED IN THE PARTIAL SHADE. She wasn't ready to go home and face an entire village of friends who were going to be told they were getting a good deal out of being forced to move. They'd probably believe it and start packing. On the other hand, they might cry foul and kill the messenger.

She needed some perspective. If it wasn't the middle of the night back home, she'd call Cam and see if he could help her out. Despite their complicated history, he was a great resource.

She had a lot of friends in Nkuve, but none with any influence. She ran through her list of contacts. Dawkin had a strict hands-off policy for getting involved in local politics. So did most of the folks she'd known back in her Peace Corps days and the few she knew in the missionary community. SJ lived close by, but she was pretty sure his village had already relocated. Normally, she would go to the chief, but that was obviously a closed door. On a whim, she dialed Jason's number. He might be new around here, but he was levelheaded *and* he clearly had connections.

She listened to the phone ring on the other end of the line.

"Hello?"

She loved the sound of good old American English. In English, she could be herself, speak her mind without worrying whether she was being understood or not. "Hi. Jason?"

"Speaking."

"It's Cassie."

"Oh, hi." He didn't sound as happy to hear from her as she'd hoped. "How can I help you?"

So stilted. Maybe he wasn't the right one to call after all. She cleared her throat. "Listen, I was wondering if you could help me out with something."

"What's that?"

"It's just—I'm not asking you to pull any strings or anything, but I could tell the other night that you're somebody. Government, right?"

"More like project management, private sector."

"Even better. That means you're used to solving complex problems. Well, I've got one for you."

She waited until he acknowledged her with an "Uh-huh."

"You saw my village, right? And met a couple of people."

"Sure. It was . . ." He paused for a long time before filling in the last word. ". . . informative."

"It was nuts," she said. "Everyone was reacting to the news. It wasn't a normal day for any of us. They're good people, really. You'd like them if you got to know them."

"I did like them, Cassie. I mean, I had no reason not to. What's up?"

She detected irritation in his voice. "I don't want to bug you. You're busy, I can tell."

"Who isn't? How can I help?"

"I've got to find a way to keep this stupid dam from flooding us out. There's got to be a way to stop it, you know? I'm usually an idea kind of gal. I can throw out ideas all day long. It's just focusing in on one good idea instead of a whole bunch of okay ones that gets me, you know, figuring out which are the golden ones."

"Mm-hmm." He wasn't giving answers out for free, that was for sure.

"Anyway, I was wondering if I could pitch you a few ideas and see what sticks. You can help me narrow down my thoughts to one that will work."

It took him a long time to answer. "I don't think I'm the guy for this job."

She pressed on. "Listen, I see three directions we could go with this thing—we can go through official channels to stop the dedication, we could have a legal battle, or we could go all out with a grassroots protest kind of thing. I'm leaning grassroots. What do you think?"

He sighed. "I think I'm not the one you should talk to about this. I'm sorry, I've gotta go."

Did he just hang up on her? She took the phone away from her ear and double-checked that she hadn't just lost the signal.

He did. Weird.

A day ago, she'd thought he was the answer to all her problems. What had happened?

Jason closed his eyes and tipped his head back against the cushioned leather of his office chair. He'd let it go too far without telling her what he did. Now she thought of him as her confidant, not realizing that she was talking to her adversary. The only reason he was in Nkuve was to clean up the mess of the botched flooding prediction. His job was to help the people of the five affected villages transition to their new homes without too much media outcry. In that regard, he had the same responsibility to Cassie as to all the other residents, so why did it feel so much more personal?

He shook it off. It wasn't more personal. It was just that she was the only one he knew. But wasn't that the very definition of being personal?

From across the room, his coworker Emanuel asked, "Everything okay?"

Jason opened his eyes. "Yeah. Yeah, it's fine."

Emanuel, like all the local office staff Jason had met, dressed like he was working on Wall Street. He stood and buttoned his jacket. "Making progress?"

Just the thought of wearing full business attire in this climate made Jason sweat. He scratched the back of his head and exhaled. "Yeah. It's great. I've met most of the diplomats, visited the dam and the five villages. Not bad for three days' work. But it's a pretty big mess, and it has a lot of potential to blow up on us. You know what's interesting?"

"What?"

"There's this one woman who's trying to stop the project—"

Emanuel stopped him. "She won't be able to. It's too far along."

"I know. We'll push it through, but she could put a kink in it if she has as much drive as I think she does."

"A parrot might squawk, but who will take its advice?"

Jason walked to the coffee bar and poured himself an espresso. "They might listen to this one. She's a spitfire. And an American."

"Oh." The one word said it all. Anywhere you traveled, Americans had a reputation. Stubborn, yes. Opinionated, of course. Who wasn't? But Americans had an inner gear different from other nationalities. It was something to do with innovation, with not being afraid to speak up or stand out or call attention. Most of these projects were done in such remote areas, no one ever even knew about them but the people they displaced. He'd never had to displace an American before.

He was finding she was a whole different critter. She'd have not only her opinion but the moral superiority of a cause to fight for and the power of social media. Things could get sticky.

"Yeah. Oh." Jason downed the strong coffee. "That was her on the phone. She lives in one of the villages. Baba something or other."

"Kondji. Babakondji. *Kondji* just means 'place.' 'Sorry place.' Like 'sorrow.'"

Who would name their town "the sorry place"? Something sad must have happened here. Jason said, "Pretty soon we can call it Place of Awesome Fishing or Place Where Electricity Is Born. No more sorrow. These people are poor. What we're giving them is so much better than what they've got."

"Not the American."

Emanuel didn't even know there was an American until a minute ago. "What do you mean?"

"Westerners can't own property. She's probably just a renter. We don't compensate renters."

"Shoot. I hadn't thought about that." So, despite her effort to fight for her neighbors, she was the one who would be truly displaced.

Emanuel leaned on the edge of Jason's desk. "What did she want? Is she looking for a favor?"

Jason creased his brow. "That's the ironic thing. She doesn't know where I work. She's trying to get me to gang up against the ETN to stop this project. I don't think that's in my best interest, do you?"

Emanuel shook his head and chuckled. "You lucky devil. The one opponent to the project just falls in your lap, begging you to help her stop you from doing what you do? Beautiful."

Really beautiful, but not in the way Emanuel meant. "She's a pest."

"No, no, no. This is good. She really doesn't know where you work?"

"No."

"Call her back. Call her right now and offer to help in any way you can. Then you hold the cards."

"I don't know. That's not exactly playing fair . . ." The back of his neck tingled. He didn't want to deceive her.

"Who's to say what's fair? You don't have to lie, just keep not telling her the truth."

Jason's stomach knotted. "I think I should tell her."

"You can always change your mind. But she's offering you an opportunity here that you can't ignore. You're just doing your job. And if you don't use the advantage, you're shirking." He shrugged. "I'd hate to report you."

Jason glared at Emanuel. He wouldn't, would he? "Report me? For telling the truth?"

"For lack of diplomacy." Emanuel stood over him. "You are here to make this move go smoothly for people. For all of them. Not just one. Would you jeopardize all of that for the sake of this girl?"

"I don't know. I don't want to deceive her."

"Do you believe in what we are doing? Do you think people will be better off because of this dam?"

"Of course I do." That was an easy question to answer. Babakondji was just a collection of mud and grass. He was offering concrete homes, electricity, even money.

"Then all you have to do is what you've already done. Do not lie. Just do not divulge."

It was a fine line, one that Jason hated dancing along. Unbidden, a line from *Star Trek* flashed through his mind, something to the effect of considering the needs of the masses before those of individuals. In theory it rang true, but in practice it didn't sit right.

At some point he should tell her. He could keep communication lines open until the time was right.

Jason picked up the phone and pulled up Cassie's number. He swallowed the pit in his throat.

Managing problems was his job. He was just doing his job.

She picked up. "Hello?"

Jason took a deep breath. He felt Emanuel's stare cut into him. "Hey, Cassie. Sorry about that. I don't know what happened. We must have been cut off. Anyway, I'd love to hear your ideas. Can we meet somewhere to talk?"

Chapter 12

CASSIE QUICKENED HER STEPS DOWN the hill. Now that she'd arranged to meet Jason tomorrow, she didn't feel as panicked. Together they could come up with an idea that would change everything.

That was tomorrow, though. She wouldn't sit on her hands until then. She needed to get things moving, build momentum in the village, get people to see their dilemma. Once they saw the risk of inaction, they could move together in a helpful direction.

From here, Babakondji didn't look like much, just a mangy brown spot in the green landscape. Some mud houses, thatch or metal roofs, a few pots and pans. The people who laid the plans for the dam wouldn't even blink at flooding out such a place. It wasn't even big enough to make it on the map of Nkuve. When she'd looked it up on Google Earth, Babakondji was made up of blobs of green and brown, a blur of low-res images with no distinguishing features. No one cared about Babakondji except the people who lived here.

She wasn't fighting the dam for the sake of social justice or equality or anything else so abstract. She was doing it for Abla and Elli and Niko and a hundred others who would lose so much without her help.

For their sake, she had to come up with a plan. As much as she loved her people, they were not the type to generate ideas. They were more likely to take whatever came their way and accept it as fate. History had engraved futility in the hearts of the people here. It wasn't futile, though, to challenge the dam. It was a stand for justice. It was necessity.

Where the road she walked met the narrower path, she joined Benedict heading in her direction. He fell into step beside her. He shortened his steps so she could keep pace with him. "You heard?" he asked.

"Heard what? About the dam?"

He shrugged. "What else? They've given an evacuation date."

"When is it?" She hadn't been gone that long. Things were moving too fast.

"Two weeks."

Two weeks wasn't enough time. She needed more time. "Why so soon?"

"It's in the plan."

"What plan? Since when is there a plan?"

He picked a long piece of grass from beside the path and stuck it between his teeth.

Cassie looked at him. "Benedict, why don't you care?"

"I care." He didn't meet her eyes.

It could just be out of politeness, but she chose to take it as being disingenuous. "It doesn't look like it. It looks like you've already given up."

"What power do we have?"

"You have a high school diploma. You have the power of education."

"With no chance of going on to university or getting a good job. What kind of power is that? They tell us to move, we move."

She wanted to say, "What if they told you to jump off a bridge?" but that wouldn't translate in a region where the highest bridge was less than ten feet above the water. "What if they told you to plant corn before beans in the same field? Or if they told you using a mosquito net will stop you from getting malaria? Or that you must boil your water to keep your children from getting sick?" All government projects with millions poured into marketing, but very little success on the adoption level.

"That's different."

She waited for him to explain.

He shook his head a couple of times. "You Americans think the success of our crops and the health of our children is something we can control. You don't see the other forces that work against us."

Putting up a mosquito net seemed like such a small effort for a big payoff. "But moving isn't like that?"

"Where you live, in the end, doesn't matter. What matters is that you live a constant life, you do nothing to offend your ancestors, and you have many children so you won't be forgotten."

By those standards, Cassie wasn't doing well.

Benedict walked Cassie all the way home. Antoinette was in the courtyard when they arrived, arranging piles of fabric for sale at the market.

She thought Antoinette was going to spend the morning telling everyone about the chief's betrayal. Half the village should be here. Why was it only her landlord?

Cassie approached her. "How did it go? Where is everyone?" Was it possible that Antoinette hadn't been able to convince anyone at all?

Antoinette looked at her like she was crazy. "Wode?"

Cassie stopped herself. She'd forgotten the greeting. Without greeting each other properly, the conversation couldn't proceed. "Woli," she said. Most days, she enjoyed the way the long-required greetings slowed you down enough to really consider the person you were talking to, but on days like today, she'd just as soon get down to business. "Babakondjitowode?"

"Woli," Antoinette replied. *All the people of Babakondji are there.* "A few said they will come. Should I call them?"

"Yes, yes. Of course." Thank goodness. They were just waiting for her return before they gathered.

Elli was the first to arrive. Good ol' dependable Elli. Cassie already knew she could count on this close friend.

Elli's cousin Abla came next, then Komi, Niko, and Therese. With Benedict, Antoinette, and herself, Cassie counted eight people. Not exactly an army, but if you considered they represented eight families, it was a start.

Cassie pulled both her chairs outside. With her cooking stool and a long bench, there were just enough seats for everyone. She looked around the circle. Benedict was the only one in this group who had finished high school. She handed him a pen and a notebook and asked him to jot down any ideas. "Don't judge if they're good or bad. Just write down what you hear."

He accepted the task with an air of seriousness.

"I talked with the man who wrote the newspaper article and got more details about what is happening. He said the deadline to leave Babakondji is in less than a month. Benedict here says he's heard we have only two weeks."

"Where are we supposed to go? What are we supposed to do?" Abla sounded like she was about to cry.

"Cassandra will know what to do," Elli said. She looked to Cassie. "Right?"

Before she had a chance to answer, Komi said, "I do not see what is so bad about moving. It is not like we have got anything that cannot be replaced. Whatever we end up in will be better than this garbage pit."

"This *garbage pit* is home," Cassie said. "You'd leave it so easily?"

Komi spit a glob of tobacco onto the ground. It looked like a blood clot against the red earth. He wiped his mouth with his sleeve. "In a second, if they offer me a better place. I will not be staying here long anyway. I am moving to America."

Not that there was much chance it would ever happen, but he wasn't the only one who would move if he could. Most people she knew would be happy to leave this life behind for a chance at life in America, the land where they thought all good things came from. Not Cassie. She'd been there, and she knew the beauty of the simple life here was something you couldn't buy.

"How many of you want to stay in Babakondji?" Cassie asked. She put her own hand in the air.

Elli raised her hand, and Abla, reluctantly, right after her.

"Of course we will stay if we can," Antoinette said. "But if we cannot, we will adapt. We always do. I can always move back north. I will wait and see."

Niko and Benedict both piped in that this was a good plan. Wait and see. That's what they should do.

"What about the chief?" Cassie asked. "He betrayed you."

Antoinette said, "He did leave. But maybe he did not betray. If he told the truth, he is going to prepare jobs and houses for us. We will see."

Wait and see. *Mia note kpo.* Cassie couldn't understand this approach at life. If you wanted to make your own future, you had to *do* something. She, for one, could not sit back and see what would happen.

"We need to do more than just wait and see. If I organize a plan to help us fight the dam, will you help me with it?"

As expected, Elli and Abla agreed right away. Bless them. At least she had a couple of faithful friends.

Komi spit again. "Do you not think the ETN is going to help us move into a better place? They are building a cité for the other villages—paved streets and real houses with electricity and everything. We should see if they will do the same for us."

"What about your parents? And your grandparents? Are they going to want to move? What are they saying about the flooding?"

Benedict said, "My father says he will wait and see."

They would still be waiting when the water came crashing through their doors at this rate. Someone needed to do something.

Someone was her.

Chapter 13

A VERVET MONKEY EYED CASSIE from his perch along the restaurant's half wall. A tight collar around his waist attached to a chain that anchored him out of reach of the table.

Cassie eyed him back.

"Cute, huh?" Jason said. He pointed a French fry at the monkey.

The little guy chattered at him.

"From a distance," Cassie said. She snatched a fry off Jason's plate. "They're thieves, though. And clever. I wouldn't put it past him to get out of that collar. He'd be on the table in a second."

"That'd be okay."

She snatched another fry. "I used to have one."

"A monkey?"

"Yeah. When I first moved here. King Kong. She was smaller than this one, but she could make a mess with the best of them." When she'd found out she was being posted in West Africa, getting a pet monkey was at the top of her list of things to do when she settled in.

"You don't have her anymore?"

"I accidentally locked her inside while I was out for the day. She tore through everything I owned. I don't think there was a single thing left in my house that wasn't chewed, torn, or pooped on."

He stared at the monkey with a more critical eye. "So you found her a new home."

"Old one, actually. I took her to the jungle and let her go. I just hoped that was her habitat. I was done with her."

"And you think she can take care of herself in the wild?"

"At that point, I didn't really care. I didn't know anyone to give her to, not in the village. Anyway, she took off into the woods without looking back. Didn't even say good-bye. She was that glad to see me go."

Jason pushed his plate of fries to the middle of the table. "Help yourself," he said. "I've had all I want."

She took one more and nibbled on it. It tasted of peanuts. She reached for the ketchup bottle. The label said Heinz, but the bottle had been refilled many times in its life. The stuff in there now was an orangish, watery mixture. No thanks.

Jason leaned back in his chair. "You didn't call me here to talk about monkeys and French fries. At least I hope you didn't."

Cassie smiled. "No, of course not." She took a deep breath. She had the perfect story to reel him in. "Did you know I'm Irish?"

"Shocker."

"My great-great-grandparents crossed the pond, as they say, a hundred years ago. They were lucky, opened their own store and lived out the American dream. My great-grandmother, Mahmee, was born in America."

"Why the family history?"

"She was born in a brick house in St. Louis. She died in the same house eighty-nine years later. I think it was in the forties or fifties that a big developer came through and knocked down her neighborhood to put up bigger, better apartment buildings."

"So they knocked her house down after she died?"

"No, no. This was even before she got married. She was a holdout. You know what that means?"

Jason picked up a fry and tossed it to the monkey, who caught it in midair and stuffed it in his cheeks. "Tell me."

"She wouldn't sell and she wouldn't move. So they built the huge new apartment buildings all around her and left her house alone."

"Like that movie."

"What movie?"

"*Up*. The cartoon. Remember?"

"I don't think so." She didn't get to the movies much.

"It's about this old man who refuses to sell his little house when the skyscrapers start going in around him. He attached a bunch of balloons to the house to fly away to the Amazon so they wouldn't knock it down."

She stared at him. What did balloons and the Amazon have to do with anything? "Anyway, Mahmee was my hero. I took a picture of her place before they tore it down. A little brick house squished in between two huge glass buildings." She couldn't recall the old place without tears of pride springing to her eyes.

"We're not really talking about your grandmother, are we?"

"Mahmee's house wasn't like anything else around it. I bet those developers thought she was a smudge on their pristine new project. But to me, she was the sweet breath of home nestled in the armpit of so-called progress. They offered her money. They offered her land, moving expenses, trips. But they couldn't offer her what she really wanted."

"Which was?"

"To stay home and be left alone."

"And you see yourself as the Mahmee of your village?" He leaned forward in his chair.

She shook her head. "I see my village as Mahmee's house of Nkuve. None of us are going to move. The whole village stays."

"What about the water? If it rises, there's nothing you can do to stop it."

"Which is why we have to stop it before the water gets that high."

He tossed a fry to the monkey.

He caught it with both hands and stuffed the whole things in his cheeks. He grinned at them.

Jason said, "Are you serious?"

"I'm more mule headed'n Mahmee. If she dug her heels in, I'll dig in to my neck." She meant it, too.

"All by yourself?"

"With anyone who will help me. I've got a core team behind me, and we'll have more people on our side as soon as reality hits."

Jason swallowed. "How many on your team?"

"Twenty, thirty?" It was an inflated number, but she knew she could recruit that many.

"And where do I come in?"

"All you have to do is bow to my every whim," she said with a grin.

He pursed his lips, leaned back, and crossed his arms.

She held up her hands and laughed. "Just kidding. I'm kidding," she said. "I need an outside ear, someone who's objective and not in the middle of this mess. Can I bounce ideas off you?"

His shoulders relaxed, and he smiled for the first time since they'd sat down. "Bounce away."

When she first asked him to be a sounding board, Jason was relieved. He'd been afraid she was going to ask him to take arms against himself, but she just wanted an American ear to empathize with her. The more he listened, the more she sucked the warm fuzzies out of him. She was talking to him like a confidant. She had no idea he was a spy.

"So, here's my idea," she said. She moved the plate of mushy fries to the next table and opened a composition book.

The monkey, now in reach of the fries, hopped onto the table and turned his back to Cassie and Jason, protecting his find from predators.

"The dam is here, right?" She drew a curved double line and then some wiggly lines for the river. "And they're saying it's going to reach here." She tapped the napkin with the tip of her pen where her village would be.

The barracuda he'd had for lunch felt like it was gnawing through his stomach from the inside out.

"That means the lake will be this big." She drew the lake as a circle.

He fought the urge to grab her pen and redraw the lake as a multifingered blob.

"But it was only supposed to be this big." She redrew the shoreline.

He didn't want to hear her ideas, didn't want to get sucked deeper into his betrayal. He should tell her and get it over with . . . now, before it got any worse.

He held up a hand. "Let me stop you there for a minute." How should he say it? He should just blurt it out and then deal with the consequences.

A text alert chimed from his phone. He looked at the screen.

Pierre A. The guy from the paper. Saved by the bell.

"I'm sorry," Jason said, rising from his chair. "I need to get this."

"No problem." Cassie grabbed her own phone to scroll through while he walked away. He wandered across the restaurant to the low wall that held the rustic outdoor shelter back from the sea. The white of rolling, roaring waves underlined the deep gray green of the sea. From here, you could sail straight south and not hit anything until you ran into Antarctica.

Jason read the text from Pierre.

Doing a story on reactions to the dam. Can we talk?

He'd have to schedule it later in the afternoon. After he finished with Cassie, he was planning to swing by the dam on his way out to Babakondji to make initial offers. He texted Pierre his time frame and walked back to the table to wrap things up with Cassie. Now that he'd decided to tell her, he needed to get it over with.

As soon as she saw him, she stood and tossed her phone in her backpack. "Listen," she said. "I've got to go. Sorry to have to leave in a hurry. Can we pick this conversation up again soon?"

Jason, whiplashed by how quickly the mood of the lunch had turned, agreed. It was the easiest thing. He would tell her next time. "Yeah. Of course."

She walked beside him to his car, the only one in the small gravel lot.

"Well, bye," she said. "My taxi will pick me up here." Her nose wrinkled when she squinted in the sun.

"Are you heading home?" he asked. He was hoping he wouldn't run into her in the village.

"Not right away. Something just came up."

Good. He reached out to shake her hand.

She ignored his handshake and gave him a short, tight hug.

He didn't know how to react. He wanted to hug her in return, but it made him feel like Brutus stabbing his best friend Caesar in the back. He wasn't betraying her exactly. It was just too complicated to explain everything right now. Next time, though. For sure.

She stepped away and looked up at him. She might as well have had two swords sticking out of her eyes.

He should just tell her now and have it over with. She'd hate him forever, but at least she'd hate him for who he was, not like him for who he wasn't.

A taxi van rolled to a stop at the edge of the road.

"That's my ride. I can't thank you enough. It's good to know I've got at least one person I can count on," she said, twisting the swords. "It's been tough, you know? But we'll make it through. Well, anyway, bye."

"Bye," he said lamely.

He stood there until the van pulled out of sight.

He climbed into his own vehicle and rested his head against the steering wheel. It didn't help.

Jason glanced at his watch. He was pretty close to the dam. He really ought to get over there to drop off copies of the offers before heading to Babakondji. He pulled his company-provided map out of its sleeve and read through the detailed directions to the Central Bodo Project to help him navigate from here.

He started by heading north to Dagbo, following the road he'd traveled with Cassie when he took her home. At Dagbo, he turned east toward the river. The roads here were something else. The main paved road, with no shoulders and the middle lines faded to suggestions long ago, was bad enough. The side roads were more like dried riverbeds, pitted and trenched with flash floods during the rains and abandoned to disrepair in the dry season. After a few long miles of torturous side roads, he knew he was near the dam because the road surface changed dramatically. Freshly graded, it had been shaped with a high point in the middle that would allow rains to roll off it without damaging the surface. It was the best dirt road he'd seen in this country. The only problem was the dust. As he sped along, his tires kicked up a cloud behind him that rivaled the Dust Bowl.

A woman walked down the middle of the road, a bundle of sticks as large as a cow balanced atop her head. She didn't see him until he was almost on her.

He leaned on the horn.

She jumped. On seeing Jason's car, she leaped off the road into the scrubby grass.

He slowed as much as he could, but she gave him a dirty look as he drove by.

And no wonder. She would be caught by the cloud he pulled behind him.

"Sorry," he muttered.

He turned the bend and there she was, a giant white panel of concrete holding back the potential of a nation. As soon as they opened her turbines, she would release the power to drive these people forward. Beautiful.

This was a perfect angle for a photo. Jason pulled to the side of the road and got out of the car. He looked for the right shot. Something with the Land Cruiser in it would be great. He dashed across the road and lined up the car with the dam.

He didn't think anything of the roar of an approaching truck until it was right on him. A semi, its open trailer stacked with bags of cement for the project, barreled past. In its wake, it dragged a sandstorm. Jason clenched his eyes and mouth shut, but too late. The fine powder engulfed him, tunneling up his nose, coating his eyes and mouth, inside his ears, between his fingers.

He gathered a mouthful of saliva and spit a dark stain of moisture in the dirt at his feet. He stomped across the road to the car, hoping some of the dirt would fall off. Before getting in on the gray leather seats, he brushed his arms and legs, his pants and his shirt. He ran both hands through his hair, releasing a puff of fine powder into the air. He took off his sunglasses to wipe them down, and a glimpse of himself in the mirror made him laugh. His face was completely orange other than two circles of white around his eyes where the sunglasses had covered.

Finally satisfied he'd cleaned himself the best he could, he got back into his car and drove the last few hundred feet to the dam. He crossed the temporary bridge that spanned the diverted river. On the other side, in the wide, flat parking area that held all the heavy equipment, he pulled into a makeshift parking place. In his side mirror, he noticed a familiar figure. How many redheads could there possibly be in this land of dark skin and short black hair? Only one, he'd be willing to bet. And she was heading right for him.

He threw himself sideways across the seat to hide himself from view. As he lay there, staring up through the window, he cursed himself for his terrible reaction. He should have just gotten out and yelled, "Fancy meeting you here!" Now he was lying awkwardly in the front seat of a car. How was he supposed to explain that? He hoped he wouldn't have to.

He closed his eyes, then opened them again. Funny how even as an adult the instinct was that if you couldn't see her, she couldn't see you.

He twisted his head to where he could see out both the driver's side and the passenger's side windows. He held his breath. And waited.

How long should he stay hidden before sitting up? If he sat up too soon, she might turn around and see him. Surely by now she was gone.

He slowly sat up, enough that he could look over the parking lot. He didn't see her anywhere.

Gingerly, he turned the key in the ignition. The diesel engine grumbled to life. Jason wanted to shush it, but reminded himself that all the big equipment around here made a lot more noise than his little Land Cruiser. He could get a better angle on the reservoir from upstream anyway. He'd circle back to the dam later, when it wasn't so crowded.

In first gear, he slowly pulled out of his parking place and headed back toward the little bridge. A cement truck stood in his way. He pulled around the front of the truck and breathed a sigh of relief. She hadn't seen him.

As he crossed the little bridge, he glanced in his rearview mirror. Cassie stared at him, open jawed, from across the parking lot.

Chapter 14

CASSIE SQUINTED INTO THE CLOUD of dust left by the white Land Cruiser peeling out of the parking lot. It sure looked like Jason, but it couldn't be. He'd said he was heading back to the office. Kutome was in completely the opposite direction from here.

It sure did look like him, though. And his car.

No, she told herself, every NGO in the country had cars like that. There were plenty of other yovos around with thick dark hair and the exact same shirt he'd been wearing at lunch. Right?

She shook her head. She turned around and walked toward the dam, then turned back around and stared after the Land Cruiser.

It couldn't be him.

She turned around again. Pierre would be calling her in a little while, and she didn't have a story worth telling yet. Time to get things rolling.

It looked like construction on the dam was already finished. From here, the top ran straight across to the other side of the valley, a thick white stripe across a green, brown, and red canvas. And soon, she supposed, they would add deep blue to the scene.

A handful of workers lounged on the grass near the top of the dam. All men, most wore khaki pants, but no shirts or shoes.

"Yo-vo," one of them called in that singsongy voice that made her crazy.

She ignored the taunt, like she always did. She would answer to her name. Or to a polite address like *mademoiselle* or even *Mama*. But not to *yovo*. She made eye contact with the one worker who wasn't lying down. "Where is the office?"

He picked a long stalk of grass and slid one end between his teeth. "There," he said, indicating the general direction with the nod of his head.

On the other side of the dam stood an old shipping container. It must have been converted to an office.

"How do I get there?" Construction might be near completion, but she didn't relish walking in the shadow of such a massive block of concrete.

"Cross the top."

On top? That wasn't better. A newly worn path led to the apex of the dam. They had placed bases for a handrail, but it was unfinished. Nothing to hold on to, just a long, narrow sidewalk a thousand feet high. Not really a thousand, she told herself, but it might as well be.

"Thanks." She approached the dam. On one side, the ground below was dry. On the other, a small pond had formed far below, a pond that would gather more and more water until it became a long lake. Today it wasn't much more than a puddle. And it was really far down there.

The world started to spin. She took a step away from the edge. She knew she was safe from falling, but she didn't want to test the theory.

She looked to the other end of the dam. It was pretty far. Maybe she didn't need to talk to anyone here after all. Even if she talked to the guy in charge, what could she learn that she didn't already know?

Maybe she should go home and come back to the dam another day. Maybe she could cross below the dam and climb the hill downstream so she wouldn't have to do a tightrope act.

Maybe she was being an idiot. If she could walk down a sidewalk without falling off, surely she could walk across this dam.

"Hey, yovo! You scared?" the man behind her taunted her.

That did it. If anything could prod her forward, it was being called chicken by a mob of catcallers. She'd show him.

She stepped onto the dam.

Don't look down. Just look ahead. It's as easy as walking down the street.

She chose her steps carefully, walking as straight a line as she could down the middle of the crest.

Halfway across, she let her eyes wander down the dam's face. The ground shifted. She took a deep breath and forced herself to take another step. She stopped and closed her eyes. Well, that was just stupid. Closing her eyes was not going to get her across to safety. She turned carefully to look behind her. It was just as far to go back as to go forward. Going back was not the solution. It never was.

She took another step.

"Yovo!" The voice compelled her forward.

Jerk.

She forced her way forward. Step after step, a little quicker with each one. Like riding a bicycle, if she built up enough speed, she could find her balance. She counted aloud how many steps it took—eighty, eighty-five, ninety. She built up speed.

Just don't look down.

Her feet hit solid earth. The hard, red clay felt like home. She would have leaned down to kiss it if she wasn't acutely aware of the group of guys on the other side watching, judging, waiting to tease her again on her return trip.

She didn't want to think about the return, not yet anyway.

The retired shipping container sat in a patch of grass several yards away. The original color and logo had been painted over with bright green. A window and door had been rough cut into the side of the rectangular room. It reminded her of the bread oven project she'd tried to get started using metal barrels. That one didn't take off because people in her village wanted to use the barrels she bought as water storage, not as ovens.

A tall, thin African man in full business attire came out of the container's door. He headed toward Cassie at the top of the dam.

She wiped her hands on her skirt and then reached her right hand toward him in greeting. "I am Cassandra," she said.

"Emanuel Gbedegbe. Pleased to meet you," he replied. He looked African, but he sounded French. He must have been educated overseas.

"Can I talk to you for a minute?"

He waved her off. "I am very busy." He didn't even give her a chance to say what she wanted to talk about before he was past her and crossing the dam.

Rather than chase him onto that death trap, she made her way to the container. Should she knock or just let herself in? She stood on a woven mat outside and debated.

Finally, she did what the locals would do.

She clapped her hands together. "Agoh," she called.

She heard shuffling inside.

She called again. "Agoh."

"Ame."

With permission to enter, she stepped through the door. Half the container had been turned into a construction office. One whole wall was covered by a bank of filing cabinets. On top sat several hard hats in various colors and ages. Most looked like they'd had something fall on them more than once.

One wall was covered with plans, presumably of the dam, and maps of the flood zone.

A young woman sat at a desk, watching Cassie look at the room. She wore Western business attire—well, almost Western—a mustard-yellow sports coat and bright red blouse. McDonald's colors. Beneath the desk, Cassie caught a glimpse of pointy-toed shoes in matching yellow. If she had to guess, she was pretty sure the woman was wearing a pencil skirt, but she couldn't see from here. Cassie had never understood why anyone here would want to adopt the Western business style of dress, a fashion that had been developed in countries that had winter.

Cassie looked down at her own choice of clothing, an untucked T-shirt, a long skirt, and some sandals. The more airflow, the better.

"Can I help you?" The young woman smiled. Her teeth shone white against her dark skin.

"Yes," Cassie said. "I hope so. I'd like to talk to someone in charge."

"Do you have an appointment?" She looked at her calendar, as if she didn't know.

"No, I was passing by and thought I'd stop. There's a problem. I really need to talk to your boss."

The secretary picked up her phone and put it to her ear, but she didn't dial. Instead, she fiddled with her earring. After a few seconds, she said, "I am sorry. He is not in."

Cassie wasn't falling for that one. "I can wait."

"Perhaps you would like to make an appointment?"

"No, I want to see someone today. It's quite far out of my way to come here." Not to mention having to cross the top of the dam again. "Isn't there anyone on-site I can speak with?"

The secretary put the phone down and stopped pretending to speak into it. "Concerning what?"

"Concerning the villages that just found out they are in the flood zone." Cassie walked to one of the maps and looked at it. She found her tiny village of Babakondji, clearly situated within the blue marked on the map. "We are being told we have to leave our homes, but we will be taking recourse. I'd love to speak to someone about next steps."

The secretary stood and came around the desk. Pencil skirt, sure enough. "You'll need to speak with Mr. Birkman. He works off-site. Would you like to make an appointment?"

Cassie mentally filed the name Birkman. She looked back at the map. On closer inspection, she could see a previous line that had been scribbled over with the blue marker that filled the floodplain, a line that left Babakondji on dry ground. She snapped a photo of the map, zooming in on the adjusted line.

"You cannot take pictures in here. This is private property." The secretary's tone was clipped.

"Funded by public monies." Cassie had the same feeling she did when an arbitrary person stretched a rope across the road so they could stop traffic. This woman was playing the power card. Well, two could play that card. She walked across the room to a low black leatherish chair. When she sat down, she sank back. She found it too deep and too low and too plasticky to be at all comfortable or dignified. She wriggled her way upright and sat on the edge of the cushion. "I'll wait," she said. "He'll be back today sometime?"

"You can't just wait here. I don't even know when he'll be here. His office is in Kutome."

"Then call him. Tell him I will wait."

Reluctantly, the woman picked up her phone again. She spoke in a very low voice, but to Cassie's ear, it sounded like she had switched from French to English. Mr. Birkman must be either Ghanaian or Nigerian. It figgered.

The secretary went back to her side of the desk and lowered herself onto her rolling chair. "He didn't pick up his phone. I left him a message, but I'm not sure when he'll get back to me. You might as well go."

Cassie couldn't leave without some kind of news to share with Pierre. "Can't I at least speak with him?"

"If he is not answering his phone, how can you speak with him? I will give you his number, and you can try him later."

Cassie left with a handwritten phone number in hand and a photo of the redrawn lines in her phone. It wasn't enough to call Pierre about unless she wanted her story to be "Project Manager Not in Office."

She couldn't bring herself to cross the top of the dam again. Maybe when it was complete with handrails and a nice sidewalk, but not before. She scrambled down the slope to the bottom of the valley on the upstream side of the dam. The pond, so far, was less than twenty feet across and only a couple of inches deep. She walked around it to the other side. Soon they'd stop the river's diversion and shunt all the water this way. Hard to believe this shallow pool would keep growing and deepening over the next few weeks until it reached the height of the dam, nearly a hundred feet overhead.

She ran her hand along the bottom of the dam. It was coated in a layer of pure cement, smooth and bright, the same finish as on her floor. She hoped they'd laid this cement on much, much thicker. Her own floor was pitted with holes that formed as tiny impurities in the under layers floated to the surface and broke through the paper-thin cement. Surely they would take better care with a project this huge.

Cassie stepped out of the dam's shadow into the midafternoon sun. The heat hit her like she'd opened an oven. She stepped back a couple of paces into the shade. This time of day, finding a bit of shade without standing directly under a tree or a roof was unusual. This dam must offer constant shelter from the sun's rays.

Maybe she should pull up a chair and stay awhile.

An idea started forming of how she and her group could make an impact. Pulling up a chair was a great idea.

Not just her own chair, but a bunch of others as well. Cassie would round up her friends, and they'd all sit down for a strike.

Chapter 15

IN THE TAXI ON THE WAY HOME, Cassie texted two photos to Pierre, the one of the redrawn lines and one she'd snapped of the water collected at the base of the dam.

I've got your story. When do you want to talk?

He texted back immediately.

What is it?

Sit-down strike. More later.

Interesting. Call me with details.

With Pierre and his article in her pocket, all she needed was a group of people who believed as strongly as she did that Babakondji was worth fighting to save. That was the easy part.

She'd start with Elli, of course, who would help with anything she asked. When she got to Babakondji, she found Elli in front of her parents' house, where she still lived, shucking goober peas.

"Afternoon, friend," Cassie said. She dropped her backpack and sat down, reaching immediately into the pile of peanuts to help shell them.

"You will drink water?" Elli asked. Without waiting for an answer, she went to the clay pot and dipped a generous cupful of water into a stainless steel mug. She gently put her lips to the cup to take a sip before offering it to her friend.

Cassie took the cup and drank it all. It didn't bother her anymore that Elli drank before her. Once she realized where the custom came from, a throwback to the days when people were poisoning their visitors right and left, she stopped worrying about germs. Nothing an antibiotic and regular deworming couldn't take care of. The cost of friendship was worth the risk.

Cassie handed the empty cup back to Elli, who set it back on the clay jar.

Fabrice played in the dirt nearby. He ran to Cassie and climbed onto her lap. He petted her hair with his thin fingers.

"You woke up well?" Elli asked.

"Very well, and you?"

"I woke up. Your mother?"

"She woke up."

"Your father?"

"He woke up."

Now that they'd established everyone was awake (for hours) and alive, Elli asked why Cassie had come. "Gbo nye fa?"

Cassie looked down at Fabrice. He still had the potbelly, the sticklike legs, the red hair, all the signs of kwashiorkor. "He's taking the vitamins I brought?" she asked.

"Of course," Elli said.

"He needs meat and vegetables. I will bring you some."

"Thank you." Elli didn't try to pretend she didn't need the help.

"I visited the dam today," Cassie said. She set Fabrice on the ground and watched him dig in the dirt with the end of a sharp stick.

"You saw it? What's it like?"

"Like a great white wall. Bigger than anything you can imagine. I have an idea, but it's going to take a lot more people than we already have."

"How many?"

"As many as we can find. We need to strike."

By the panic on Elli's face, she knew she'd chosen the wrong word again. She'd used the French word *grève*. She rephrased. "Not a strike . . . more like a protest."

"What's the difference?" Elli asked. "Both are a bad idea."

She searched for another way to communicate the thought. She hit her elbow against her side like little kids did to say they were willfully disobeying. "Mia gbe." *We will refuse.*

With that explanation, Elli relaxed a bit. Then she shook her head and clicked her tongue. "I don't think we can find many who will join us. The offers came today."

"What do you mean?"

"Some men came from the ETN to give us our choices."

So soon? "They came today?" The one day she left the village to try to delay the flooding, they swooped in with their offers. She should have been here. "What happened? When did they leave?"

"Not long before you got here. They called us all together for a village meeting to explain our choices. Then they talked to each landowner individually. Chief Gbeze was there. And that friend of yours."

"The chief?" He was not her friend. She hoped he would run away and never return.

"He is helping with the negotiations."

Cassie was more concerned about the people who were still here than the skunks who had left. "What about the people who were gone?"

"Most people were here. They are coming back in a few days for our answers."

"So, what's the offer?"

Elli looked at her feet, weathered by a lifetime of working the land and walking either barefoot or in flimsy plastic flip-flops. "They are replacing our village with a new one on the other side of the hill. They already started building, some weeks ago. If we move there, we will get a house and land and electricity and running water. Or we can take the money instead and move wherever we want. It is a lot of money, a generous offer."

Of course she would think it was a generous offer. She came from a family who lived hand to mouth, depending on the passing of the rains and the warmth of the soil. Any amount of money would sound generous. Cassie doubted Elli had any idea of the value of the offer.

"How much?" she asked.

"Two and a half million for the house and the land. They will pay us for our crops and our trees, too, but I do not know that amount."

"For your trees?"

"Anything over four meters is one price, and anything under four meters is another price. Oh, and they will pay us the cash value of our crop from the land for the next three years while we get resettled."

Cassie took out her phone and punched in the numbers. "So what are you going to do?"

"My brothers want to take the money, but my parents think we should take the land. What do you think?"

"There are always hidden details." Cassie pressed the equal button. That number couldn't be right. Four thousand dollars? For a house and land? She put the numbers in again and came up with the same number. "You said two and a half million?"

"Yes. And the money for the trees. I have not counted, but we probably have over a hundred. It could add up."

That amount couldn't be right. It would sound like a windfall to a subsistence farmer, but the money could be easily squandered away. The total compensation for this family was less than her own father's monthly take-home pay. Much less. "I don't think that offer is right. They've got to offer you more."

"What about the house and land? It's a fair trade, isn't it? They would give us a replacement, plus money to live off. Do you think we should ask for more?"

More than $4,000? "Yes. Much more. Ten times more."

Elli blurted out a laugh. "Ten times? Ha!"

"I'm not kidding. I think you should ask to be able to stay. Or at least they should compensate you much more generously. What about the others? Are they accepting the offers?"

"I know some have already signed the papers. The first one to sign was actually handed his cash in front of everyone. I have never seen so much money before."

"Who took the money?"

"Benedict. He practically ran up to get it."

Benedict? She couldn't believe it. He was so smart, maybe the smartest one among the young adults. Maybe being smart and being shrewd were two different things. "I think that was a very foolish decision. Where can you buy a house and farm for so little?"

"So little? It was a stack this big." Elli held her thumb and index finger apart three inches to show the thickness of the windfall.

The numbers were too large for Elli to comprehend. She was used to buying a hundred CFA of tomatoes, paying five hundred for a pair of shoes. Two and a half million might as well be a trillion.

Cassie shook her head.

"What?" Elli rubbed a handful of nuts together between her palms. The papery skins fell to the ground. A hen and her chicks pecked them up.

Cassie shooed the chickens away. "Have you ever heard the story of Yakobo and Esau?"

"I don't think so. Are they from near here?"

"No, no. They lived far from here and a very long time ago. They were twins."

Elli smiled at the mention of twins. Any family with twins was considered very lucky.

"Esau was the older twin and Yakobo the younger. Both boys. Esau was a very good hunter and Yakobo a very good cook. One day Esau came home from a long hunt. He was hungry, hungrier'n he had ever been before. When he got home, Yakobo was cooking a pot of red sauce."

"Deku detsi?"

"I don't know if was a palm nut sauce or not. I do know it smelled very, very good. Esau asked if he could eat some. Instead of giving his twin some of the sauce, Yakobo said he would sell it to him."

"Sell the sauce? To his own brother?" Elli dropped the naked goober peas from her hand into a plastic bowl.

"Yes. And for a very high price. In exchange for the pot of red sauce, Yakobo asked for Esau's birthright."

Elli scowled. "What does that mean?"

Cassie explained the word *birthright* a different way. "In this place, in this time, the firstborn son was given the biggest part of the parents' property when the mother and father died. You understand?"

Elli nodded. "Like my eldest brother will get more land than the rest of us."

Maybe ancient Canaan wasn't as far removed in time and place as she thought it was.

"Right. So Esau was supposed to get the most land and money when his parents died, but when Yakobo asked for his—for the right to this inheritance—Esau agreed."

"Nyawoa? For a bowl of sauce?"

Cassie shrugged. "He was hungry." She didn't have to overexplain. The story would speak for itself. If she directly said for Elli to not move for too low a price, she wouldn't be heard as clearly as through the moral of this ancient story.

Much as she hated to admit it, most of her neighbors were probably just as hungry. Would any of them even join a strike? She should explore some more aggressive options. First, she would call a lawyer, if she could find one. Second, she needed to understand the scope of the problem. To do that, she needed to acquaint herself with the Bodo River and with the dam farther upriver. If she could prove the first dam had been bad for people, it would help her prove this one would be as well. And if she found the Ngorogo Dam had actually helped people, well then, maybe she'd give up the fight.

Chapter 16

JASON OFFERED PIERRE A CUP of coffee from the office espresso machine.

The newspaperman was happy to accept. "A doppio, please."

"This late in the day?"

"A good reporter never sleeps."

"Two shots it is," Jason said, punching the buttons like a professional barista. "Milk or sugar?"

"What am I? An American?" Pierre laughed at his own joke.

Jason laughed too. Sometimes a stereotype nailed it. "How did you know I like mine sweet and milky?"

"I will never understand your country's love affair with dairy," Pierre said, accepting the strong black coffee. "Of course, you are nothing compared to the French."

Jason poured a generous drizzle of local cane syrup into his drink. "Have a seat." He held his hand out to offer Pierre a choice of chairs in the lounge area.

Pierre chose the seat with the shortest legs.

Fine by Jason. He didn't like chairs that were so low you were like a beached whale when it was time to stand up. He chose a cushioned armchair that put his eyes on level with the top of the reporter's head. "Listen, Pierre, thank you for coming to speak with me again. Your coverage on the Central Bodo Hydro Project is helping get the word out."

"It is news. It is what I do."

"Which helps me do what I do."

Pierre took a MacBook out of his briefcase and powered it on. "May we begin? I have a few questions."

"Please."

He set his phone on the table between them. "And I can record?"

"Of course."

"Last time we spoke, the newly affected villages had not yet been informed. What about now?"

Jason nodded, glad he and his team had finished this phase. "Definitely. They have all been informed through several lines of communication, not the least of which is the town meetings we had in each of those villages this afternoon."

"What was the purpose of those meetings?"

"We want to give people the opportunity to choose between several options for their future. Today, we laid out those options."

"Which are?"

"Relocation, compensation, or a combination of both."

"Tell me about the parameters of those options."

Jason felt comfortable with the offers they were making, but still his neck burned. It would be easy for an outsider to see the numbers and make uninformed judgments. Which was one reason his company and the ETN had worked out strict nondisclosure agreements for everyone to sign. "I can only address those in general terms. Every offer is different based on individual circumstances.

Basically, every adult who owns property will get an offer. We are building a village for them to move into—an upgrade with electricity and a reliable pump water source. If they own land, we will replace their land in another location and compensate them for any plants they will need to replace along with a food stipend for the next several planting seasons until their farms are established."

"So you are moving everyone to a new location?"

"Not everyone. Some might choose the buyout option, in which case they would take settlement in full and not be given house or land."

"And you trust people not to squander it?"

Jason carefully framed his answer. "We can't control how people spend the money, but we can ensure that we give a fair offer. In this case, we are offering signing bonuses because of the strict timeline. We are hopeful we can help the affected families move into suitable situations while allowing the ETN to complete its project on time. We are dealing with adults. They have options—fair options."

Pierre tapped madly at his keyboard, catching up with whatever it was Jason had said that required capturing in print as well as on the recording device. When he finished, he made eye contact again. "Tell me about the meetings. Were they well attended? Well received?"

Jason considered the question. "Yes, I'd say they were. A few people had a lot of questions. A few already made their decisions. It often goes that way. We didn't pressure anyone to choose today." The faces of the people of Babakondji flashed through his mind. The same people who had been overcome with grief last time were equally enthralled with the possibilities of a better future this time. Not everyone, of course, but most.

"What is the deadline for their decisions?"

"Those villages will be flooding by the end of the month. Ideally, we would like to help them move several days before that."

"There's no definitive date?"

"Hold on." Jason stood and went to his desk to double-check the calendar. "Decision date is March 20."

"Which is in a week?"

Jason tugged at the collar of the T-shirt under his loose button-up shirt. "Yes. One week."

Dang. That was fast. No wonder people were reeling. No wonder Cassie was in a panic. It wasn't fair, he knew, but there was nothing he could do about it. The dedication ceremony was already set. The president would be there, along with diplomats from around the region and from several of Nkuve's Western allies. You didn't just postpone an event like that. The fine people of Babakondji and the other villages would just have to make their decisions quickly.

Cassie paced back and forth on the road at the top of the hill. She might as well pitch a tent up here, as much time as she was spending waiting for phone calls to be returned. The sun had set hours ago. There were no streetlights in this part of the country, and the overcast sky obliterated any light she could hope for from the moon and stars.

It was also well past the hour when she liked to be inside, tucked safely under her mosquito net. She'd long ago given up the regular regimen of malaria prevention in favor of the less effective but more natural resignation to an occasional bout with the miserable disease. At least she'd survive her years in Africa with liver intact. And at least she could empathize with her friends and their children who couldn't afford the weekly prophylaxis.

Pierre should have called by now. Maybe he was expecting her to call him. She dialed his number, but got no response.

A few seconds later, a text chimed in.

In a meeting. Call you in a few.

Great. She hoped it would be a short meeting. She hadn't slept well in nights and was eager to get home. She strode farther up the road, feeling her way along by instinct more than anything else.

"Yovo." A man's voice nearby startled her. It always surprised her at night when people she could not see identified her by her glow. Even squinting, she couldn't see anyone.

"Good evening," she said to whoever it was.

His footsteps faded as he continued on his way without stopping to converse.

She wandered back down the road.

At last, her phone rang. "Hello?"

"Cassandra?" Pierre sounded like he had her on speaker phone. The tin can sound of his voice made it hard to understand.

"Yeah, I'm here."

"Sorry for the delay. Please tell me about this strike of yours."

She sighed. The idea that had seemed so fresh and full of possibilities this afternoon had fizzled fast when she couldn't line anyone up to participate. "It's coming together."

"When?"

"Um, this week. Friday?" Why hadn't she thought to come up with a plan before he started asking questions?

"At the dam?"

"Mm-hmm."

"And how many are you expecting?"

"Oh, lots." Which was quite an exaggeration considering she could count the people she might be able to drag there on two hands and the people who actually wanted to do it on one finger.

"That is not very specific. Is there really going to be a strike?"

"Well, the details aren't ironed out yet. I'm still pulling plans together. I'll let you know, though, when it's going to be. You won't want to miss it."

"So, no strike?" He didn't sound so much disappointed as disinterested. Without his precious story, he had no reason to report her side.

"Yes, there will be one. I promise. It's just not organized yet. I have another idea, though. I'm hiring a lawyer. A good one."

"For what?"

"To stop the dam, of course. We'll get a cease and desist to give people time to state their side."

"And what is their side?"

"That they are being unfairly forced off their land and out of their homes."

"But aren't they being compensated? The package offer I heard did not sound unreasonable."

So he'd already heard the offer. She wondered if he'd spoken with someone in one of the villages or if his only source was the electric company. His impassiveness frustrated her.

"It's not reasonable. None of this is. It's completely crazy. Who said it was reasonable? Have you spoken to my neighbors?"

"Not specifically. Do you have a couple of names of people who are upset with what they've been offered? I'd love to get their angle on things."

When Cassie lowered the phone to get the numbers of a couple of her friends, she noticed her hands were shaking. What was this feeling? She couldn't describe it as anything but fury. She wasn't the type to hold on to anger, but here she was seething and overflowing with it. She forwarded numbers for Elli, Niko, and a couple of others before she put the phone back to her ear.

"Listen, Pierre," she said, her voice quivering. "I know you aren't supposed to pick sides, but I could use some help. Just point me in some direction. Who should I talk to? Who is powerful enough to stop this thing?"

Pierre cleared his throat. He paused for a few seconds before answering with carefully selected words. "Listen, I know you want to do what's best for Babakondji. I believe your motivation is sincere, but are you sure stopping the dam is actually the best thing for your village?"

"How can it not be? If I don't stop it, the town won't even exist anymore."

"Think about it," he said. "Just think about it. But if you really feel like you need to fight, here is my advice. Normally I would suggest a political approach, but the president has already given his approval on this project. He will be at the dedication ceremony. It is an opportunity for him to show the world Nkuve is making progress. I think you are right that you should hire an attorney. I cannot promise it will make a difference. If you want the hardest-hitting lawyer in the country, you have to go with Viadji. But I am warning you, he is not cheap. He is the best and he charges accordingly."

"Viadji?" She scribbled the name on the palm of her hand. She hoped it would be legible when she got back into the light. "Oh, thank you. Thank you so much. I'll call him first thing tomorrow."

"Public knowledge," he said. "Good luck. Thanks for the names. And if you do end up pulling together a strike, please call me."

"I will," she said, thankful to have the name of a reputable attorney she could call and a reporter who was, if not in her pocket, at least willing to go there.

While she was still at the top of the hill, Cassie decided to make a couple more phone calls. She started with a video call to Cam. She half hoped he wouldn't answer, but was disappointed when he didn't. Rather than leaving him a long, complicated message after not talking to him for so long, she left him an IM asking him to text her when it was convenient for him to talk. He was likely at work now, so she expected a morning call would fit his schedule better.

Next, she needed to line up a way to see Ngorogo and get acquainted with the river. She didn't own a kayak, but her friend SJ did. He didn't even hesitate when she asked if she could borrow it.

"Sure thing! When?"

"Is tomorrow too soon?" she asked, aware that her every decision, her every action was hurried. All this time here, she'd worked on shedding the rush of Western life, but when she faced a crisis, her good ol' American self rose unbidden to the occasion. Which was just as well. It was only a few days until everyone in her village was supposed to declare a decision about whether they would accept money or housing.

"Tomorrow's great," he said. "I'll pick you up around nine. I assume you'll want a ride?"

She hadn't even thought about transport. "That would be awesome. If you can drop me at Ngorogo, I can float down as far as the dam."

"Perfect. I have a friend I can visit up-country and still be back in time to fetch you in the afternoon."

"Are you sure? That'd be great." Finally, someone willing to help her out, no questions, no complications.

She hoped a half day on the river wouldn't be a total waste of precious time.

She dreamed that night about floating down Bodo, vivid dreams like she always had on sweltering nights. Her head filled with crazy visions of hungry crocodiles and singing hippos. Hundreds of riled-up villagers lined the riverbanks, thrusting short-handled hoes into the air like dangerous weapons. She knew they wanted her to help them, but she couldn't find her paddle. She yelled to them, but they could not hear. She floated helplessly by.

The river broadened into a large, serene lake. A young boy poled his dugout canoe across her bow. He turned and grinned at her. She waved and smiled back. He looked away, and when he turned back again, his face had changed to a grotesque mask.

Cassie startled. She wanted to back away, but the lake pulled her forward. She back paddled with her hands, to no avail. Ahead she saw the dam towering over the water's surface. A tremendous grinding sound grew louder and louder. Ahead, the lake surface dipped where the hungry dam devoured giant bites of water.

The turbines!

Cassie dipped her palms in the water and pushed backward against it with all her might. If she was a stronger swimmer, she would have abandoned her tiny boat and tried to swim to safety. She cast about, looking for a pole or a log to jam into the ravenous jaws. Nothing.

The kayak tipped its nose down toward the turbines.

Chapter 17

CASSIE AWOKE WITH A START. Where was she? How did she get through the turbines? Her eyes adjusted to the dark. She was sitting up in bed in her rented room. Not on the river. Not yet.

She lay back on her mat and closed her eyes. No need to panic. She'd be safe on her river trip. There was nothing to fear, but the unease wouldn't leave her. After a few minutes, she gave up trying to sleep. She opened the shutters wide enough to see the dark blue light that preceded the dawn. Soon it would be light enough to feed the chickens and sweep the walk. Such menial tasks would occupy her until SJ arrived.

She checked her texts to see if Cam wanted to talk to her before she left for the day. No word from him yet. She hoped he'd answer. He had more resources than anyone she could think of.

The morning dragged by. She was anxious to begin the day. She wasn't sure what she was looking for along the river's path, but she had a feeling it would tell her what she needed to know. Waking up at the crack of four did nothing but lengthen the eternity until her ride would come.

Despite her checking the time every thirty seconds all morning, SJ picked her up right when he'd said he would.

You could put an American in Africa, but you couldn't take away his internal clock unless he let you.

He drove the same old Toyota Corolla as when they'd served in the Peace Corps together. If possible, it was in even worse shape now than it had been then. The right front panel was lime green, the hood red, and the rest of the car an impossible shade of orange. The left fender looked like it came from a different make and model. She couldn't have been happier to see the familiar ol' rattletrap.

A bright yellow plastic kayak was strapped to the roof like a giant plantain, tied down with a complicated web of bungee cords and random bits of rope.

"Climb aboard!" SJ called through his open window.

Cassie tossed her basket in the backseat and climbed into the passenger's seat. Out of habit, she reached for the seat belt. The canvas strap had been sliced off near the rivet that held it to the body of the car. It dangled, useless for anything but a makeshift handhold.

SJ grinned. "Oh, yeah. Sorry about the belt. It got covered in grease and no one was using it anyway, so I just took it out of the way."

"No problem." Cassie knew none of the locals would use the thing. The occasional Westerner like her, though, was sure to appreciate any available safety measures. She sat back in her seat, but didn't relax. "You know where we're going?"

"Ngorogo, right? I've put in there before. It's not the prettiest part of the river."

"That's okay." She wasn't going for the scenery. "I just want to get a feel for it. I've lived here all this time, and I don't know the river at all. Here I'm trying to save it, and I don't even know it."

"Trying to save it? I thought you were trying to stop it."

She shook her head. "That's the last thing I want to do. I want to stop the people who are trying to stop it." He was right, though. If it meant the rescue of Babakondji, she'd do anything to keep the river from encroaching. "I'm worried about my village."

"You're on the flooding list, aren't you? Tough break."

"What about you? Is it affecting you?"

"Mmm," he said, shaking his head. "They moved us to our new location over a year ago when they started construction."

"Weren't you riled up?"

"About moving? Nah. Why fight the inevitable?"

Why indeed? Maybe she couldn't help it. Maybe she thought she could really make a difference. Maybe he should have thought so, too, but he didn't.

They were on a good paved road, hurtling northward at over 100 kilometers an hour, when Cassie's phone rang. It was Mr. Viadji's office, calling to set up an appointment. Cassie arranged to visit their law offices early the following morning.

SJ drove in silence for a while, letting her stew in her own thoughts. Should she give up as easily as he had? Was there hope for her and her neighbors if she gave in?

They left the dirt track and followed a pitted asphalt road, a nod to whatever progress the Ngorogo dam had brought with it. If the potholes were any indication, the aid offered was only for the short term. It's what she was afraid of.

SJ pulled to the side of the road. "This is as close as I can get you to the river. I'll help you get the kayak down to the bank. You starting down right away?"

"Nuh-uh. I'm gonna talk to a few people first. Do you want to hang out for a while?"

"Nah. I've got a couple of projects to visit. Midafternoon at the new dam, okay?"

"That should work." She'd roughed out the amount of time it would take to cover that distance in the kayak to be around three or four hours. Allowing a little extra time for the unexpected, she had a couple of hours to talk with the locals before heading downstream. She was curious what they could tell her about their experience with living in the shadow of a hydro dam.

SJ untied the last of the knots and slid the kayak to the ground. Together, they carried it to the edge of the water. The water here flowed slow and brown. SJ tucked the kayak in some bushes several feet from shore.

"Do you think it'll be safe here for a while?" Cassie asked.

"No problem." He whistled to call a boy, maybe nine or ten years old, over. "Keep an eye on my boat for me? My friend here will pay you 250 CFA when she comes back."

The thirty cents or so would more than compensate for his time. Cassie checked her pocket to make sure she had a coin. She did.

SJ trotted back to the car and returned with a life jacket. "Keep this on. The river's not deep in most places, but it gets a little treacherous in spots. Just to be safe."

Cassie took the jacket. She'd put it on later, when it looked like she would need it.

She watched him drive away until he was out of sight.

He had dropped her below the Ngorogo Dam. The river was narrow here. A concrete monstrosity rose out of the landscape. Over a hundred feet tall, it seemed like too much cement to hold back the tiny river that trickled through its spillways.

Cassie returned to the road and walked upstream. Beyond the dam, she found a dark lake. Fishing boats dotted its surface. Somewhere under those inky waters lay the remains of Ngorogo village. Its people had been moved to a location only a little higher, barely out of the floodplain. She could see the new village from here. The valley lay wide and flat. It lacked the tall coconut palms and the mature mango and orange trees that surrounded her home not far south of here. Surprising, really, considering the dam had been commissioned nearly ten years ago. You would think the land would heal itself in that amount of time.

It took her only a few minutes to walk to the new Ngorogo. The dirt here was dark and damp, nothing like the hard red clay of Babakondji. Her grandfather had always been proud of the dark soil on his farm. The blackness was a good sign. It might be more fertile than the red clay of the valley.

As a stranger entering the village for the first time, she knew she ought to greet the chief and ask his permission to be there. She didn't have time for that. She went immediately to the village well, the most likely place to find someone willing to talk. As she approached it, though, she saw that it wasn't a well at all, but a pump. The lucky people of Ngorogo had a pump. It was surrounded by a high concrete wall with a door that locked, though why you would want to block access to clean water, she couldn't fathom. The door stood open.

She stepped onto the concrete pad.

The pump itself was massive, with a levered handle that stuck eight or ten feet into the air. If you were big enough to operate it, it wouldn't take long to fill your basins.

As if on cue, a child came into the shelter of the pump. She set her basin under the spigot, shimmied up the pump, and used her own meager body weight to pull the entire lever down to the ground. She let the handle pull her into the air and lower her down again. The motion of her bending her knees and jumping forced the pump up and down and up again. A stream of clear water gushed from the spout and splashed into the enamel basin.

Cassie grinned at her.

The little girl grinned back. This child was not startled by her pale skin or fiery hair. She neither burst into tears nor sang out "Yovo!" the two reactions Cassie had come to expect.

"Is your mother home?" Cassie asked.

"Yes."

"Will you take me to her?"

The little girl nodded, but kept on pumping until her basin overflowed.

Cassie helped put the basin of water on the child's head. They only spilled a little over the lip of the heavy bowl.

The girl led her out of the circle of the pump and between some huts to her own family compound. Inside, her mother helped her child lower the heavy basin of water. Together they poured half the water into a cooking pot and placed it over a ready fire. The girl's father sat on a ledge alongside the house, sharpening a short-handled hoe. It wasn't time to till the ground yet, but as soon as the first rain came, he would be ready. It should be any day.

"Agoh," Cassie said, bowing a little to ask permission to enter the yard.

"Ame," said the mother.

The little girl quickly explained where she had found the yovo and why she had brought her home.

After a round of traditional greetings and the offer and acceptance of a drink of water, Cassie was able to ask her questions. She addressed both the parents at once, willing to hear from both. She took her time circling the topic before zeroing in on her real questions. "You've heard they are building a new dam downriver?"

The mother nodded. "We have heard." She picked up a knife and used it to start peeling a tiny purple onion.

"My village is one that they are saying will flood. We didn't know. Now we must decide quickly what to do."

A tear formed in the corner of the mother's eye.

Cassie didn't know if she was upset about the dam or if the onions stung her eyes. She kept talking. "They say they will relocate people and compensate them for their loss."

The father stopped sharpening his hoe. He laughed bitterly. "Compensate? Is that what they call it now?"

"Why? What did they call it then?"

"Whatever words they use, they are lies. They promised us new houses. This is what we got." He tapped his hoe handle against the corner of the house. A chunk of cement broke loose and tumbled to the ground. "And this is after they made improvements."

"Are these worse than the houses you lived in before?"

"Worse or better, who is to say? Cement is better than mud. Or is it?"

It seemed like a cement house would always be better than mud. "Isn't it?"

He shrugged. "Mud, we had plenty of. You lost a corner of the house in a storm, you patched it up with some dirt from the road. Now if the house falls down, what are we going to patch it with? Cement costs money. Look at this."

He led her out of the compound gate and across to the neighbor's house. The whole structure had crumbled, as if the ground sank beneath it and tore the concrete blocks apart. "This is the house they gave us. The choice was either to get your house replaced and some land given to you or to take a settlement in money. If you took the house, the deal was a new house in the valley, the same amount of land you gave up, and enough money to live off for three years. If you took the money, they gave you no land, no house. To some, the money was so much, they thought they could live on it forever."

"And you?"

"I went to high school. I know my math. With no home and no land, money goes fast. So I took the house, but I don't know if I made the right choice."

"Why not?"

"The people who took money got it all in one lump sum. Some of them squandered it. Some of them spent it. But some took the money and bought property farther from the river. They built houses of mud. They planted their crops and they are doing okay. But those of us who took the houses are struggling."

"How so?"

"The houses are cheaply made, but not cheaply repaired."

The shoddy workmanship was evident, even to her.

"And the land is no good. Before, we could grow everything. We were near the river. The floods would bring rich soil to the land. Corn, beans, yams, peanuts, anything you can think of would grow on my farm. I used to get three ears of corn per stalk."

"Not anymore?"

"Now I am lucky to get one. The ground here is full of water that comes from underneath. It rots the roots. There is no nutrition in this soil. We have to buy fertilizer—that is another expense—to make anything grow here at all."

"But the soil is dark. I thought that was good."

"Not for us. It grows nothing. There is no life in it."

"So, the houses are junk, the land is dead. But surely they gave you the money they promised?"

He dug his hoe tip into the hard dirt. "Three years, they said. Three years of money enough to pay for food. Long enough to plow new land, establish new crops. The first month, they gave us money, barely enough for the food we required."

"Not enough," the mother piped in. "The children were hungry, remember?"

"Almost enough," he said. "We did not know. We had always grown our own food. Now we depended on the market. Everyone did, so the prices went up. And, yes, the children were hungry, but when are they not?"

Cassie didn't have kids, but she knew it was true.

The father continued. "The second month, we waited for our money. When it did not arrive, we went looking. There is no money, they said. You are not children, they said. You must learn to feed yourselves, they said. As if we did not already know how to do just that before they tricked us into moving."

"But they promised."

"What is a promise? It is only a way to control us. Once they had what they wanted—our land and our homes—why should they care for us? And now we are ruined. Hungry, poor, with no future because our land will not care for us. We are stuck here, waiting to die."

"How long has it been?" Cassie asked. "Ten years, no?"

"No, no." He clicked his tongue. "Only eight. But eight long years with no hope that ease will shorten the next ones."

"No hope," the mother said. She dropped the onion slivers into the boiling water. With a palm branch fan, she blew air on the flame to wake it up. "We used to be famous for our cassava flour. Cassava grew on our farm even when we didn't plant it. We would eat all we wanted and sell the rest as flour. Here, we cannot grow cassava. The ground will not give it to us."

The father ran his finger along the edge of his hoe, testing its sharpness. "It will not. The land holds water that drowns the roots."

"So, what we used to sell, we cannot make here. And even if we could, who would buy it? Everyone is as poor as we are. Everyone has lost everything."

"What about the electricity?" Cassie asked. Large power lines went right past the village, but not to it. She looked for wires overhead, but found none.

He stood and spit on the ground. "Another promise, another lie. Why should they bring us power if they do not even finish building our houses? This huge dam does nothing but make electricity day and night. But do we see any of this power? Of course not. They send it far away through the wires you see overhead. We hear them buzzing at night and tell ourselves this is the sound of money flying through the air over our heads. Someone uses this power, someone takes in the money. But we receive only suffering."

The mother added, "And disease. Don't forget disease."

"What do you mean?" Cassie asked. The dam shouldn't have anything to do with sickness.

"We used to have a well. The water would filter through the sand to give us clean drinking water."

"But you have the pump."

"When it works. Yes, when it works we have clean water. When it does not, we walk to the dam to fetch our water. The water there is still. It makes our children sick. But today, today the pump is working. So, in that sense, today is a good day."

A good day, Cassie realized, was relative. She thanked the family and let herself out. She would need to start paddling soon in order to reach the new dam in time to meet SJ.

Just outside the gate, a middle-aged man fell in step beside her. He hung back to her pace, like he had something he wanted to say. His loose pair of swim trunks were held up by a knotted length of rope. Other than that, he wore only a pair of rubber sandals fashioned out of an old tire.

"I could not help overhearing," he said. "You have questions about the dam?"

He was old enough to remember.

Cassie was happy to ask him questions. "Many. Was this the plan? Is this what they said would happen?"

"We saw the plans before we made our choice. We saw them and we agreed. But after they had our names on their papers, they went ahead with other plans, ones that left us living in mud. Our lives are under those waters. I wish we could get them back."

"What do you mean?"

"Our children have gone. There is nothing to hold them here. The land they were promised by our families, generations of farmers, is barren. They have gone to find work in the cities. My own son has gone to Ghana. What is he going to find there? He may make his way, but far from us, far from his people and his land."

"Ghana is not that far." *Far*, she realized, was another relative term.

"Our land is gone, our homes, and our children. Now we only wait to die."

His defeat was total. Cassie didn't understand why he didn't struggle against it. Of course there was no hope if everyone just lay down and took it. They were so used to taking the word of people they thought held the power, they could not imagine outside the world as they had always known it.

She had the gift of being able to see their plight from the outside.

She was coming to see herself as a prophet. As much as she hated that her differences made her stand out, she was starting to understand how her ability to look in on life in Babakondji from the outside could be a gift to its people. They were so immersed in their own culture, they couldn't see how it held them back.

Certainly today had given her clarity. The ETN might promise houses and land, but Ngorogo knew the truth—that the promises were thin and empty.

Whatever she had to do to keep Babakondji from becoming the next Ngorogo, she would do it.

Chapter 18

CASSIE LEFT NGOROGO ANGRY. The ETN had tricked those people into moving, just like they were doing in Babakondji. She couldn't stand the thought of Koffi trying to farm a swamp, of Antoinette's new home crumbling around her, of little Fabrice wasting to nothing.

Cassie tipped the front of her kayak into the water, waded in up to her knees, and climbed into the little plastic watercraft, eager to get home and tell everyone what she'd seen. "Car on water," the locals called it, this and any other type of boat. An airplane was a "car in the air." Their lives were as simple as their vocabulary. Her friends had no idea what was about to hit them. Offer them a little money in exchange for their mud house, of course they were going to take it without seeing their future play out in front of them. Not that they were stupid, far from it. But when you'd spent your whole life playing by the rules, and someone changed not only the rules but the whole game, you were at a disadvantage.

She thrust the tips of her paddle into the water to back herself up. She knew she should practice a little to get comfortable first, but Babakondji called her. She needed to get there and start putting things right. She pointed downstream. The paddle blades sliced through the water like knives in softened butter, propelling her forward with each stroke. A first-time kayaking trip with no experience and no guide wasn't the smartest thing she'd ever done, but it wasn't the dumbest either. The Bodo wasn't Niagara Falls, after all, nor the Mississippi, the Amazon, or the Nile. She'd never heard of anyone getting injured along the Bodo except that one guy who'd come to her door claiming his rash was caused by a hippo spitting on him. Nothing a little triple antibiotic ointment and a good snicker wouldn't fix.

As she gained confidence in her ability to steer, Cassie dipped her paddles in the water and rowed forward with a steady rhythm. The current swept her downstream. On both sides of the water, family farms skirted right up to the banks—rows of corn or pineapple, stately coconut palms, bean vines that climbed and covered everything like kudzu. A monkey screeched at her from the branch of a mango tree.

Just ahead, she should reach the hippo pools. All the years she'd been in Nkuve, she'd never seen the hippos. Farmers in the area complained that the monstrous beasts would rise from their watery beds at night to trample and ravage the fields. But most people, like Cassie, had never taken the time to hunt them out and see them while they rested. But then, most people in Babakondji had never seen the ocean, a mere hour's drive away.

She looked, but didn't see them. Disappointed, she kept paddling. But wait. She realized the round rocks breaking the surface were their backs, nostrils, and heads. She back paddled to keep the river from taking her past them too quickly. The gentle curve of a great gray back, the flick of an ear, a snort and a chuckle. If you weren't looking for them, it would be easy to miss these great beasts who could hide themselves under the surface of the river. She took a picture in her mind, hoping to hold this moment as a special memory, the day she floated past the hippos.

Something about these giants held her there. Either the hippos had no idea she was in the water with them or they simply didn't care. But something held her, some intangible tie to the land and the past. This area should stay as it was. Progress would ruin it like it had ruined Ngorogo.

"Don't worry," she said aloud. "We're going to save the river for you."

The closest one opened his mouth wide, revealing four huge, comical teeth. He closed his jaws and sank below the surface.

The noise of rushing water took her attention from these last big animals. It was the sound she'd hoped for, the sound she feared. She rounded a bend and caught a glimpse of the river continuing in a long, brown ribbon across the green landscape. It ran flat and slow, but at a noticeably lower elevation. Between here and there, she'd have to descend. And that meant rapids.

Rapids, she reminded herself. Not a waterfall. There were no waterfalls on the Bodo, but it didn't reassure her. It wasn't like the cartoons where you'd suddenly find yourself at the top of a roaring cascade. It was more like floating the Buffalo back home. Just point downstream and let gravity do the rest. She struggled into her life jacket and snapped it around her.

There's no feeling like reaching the edge of placid water, hanging an eternity on the lip as you stare into the tumbling white water below. Cassie imagined it would feel like balancing on the horizon of an infinity pool. A vague memory of last night's dream flashed through her mind, the sensation of being sucked down, down into the spinning turbine. When she got close enough to see over the edge, though, it was nothing like an infinity pool that gently dropped the excess liquid into a drain a few inches below. It wasn't as scary as the dream, but almost. This was a serious drop into a churning mass of white-capped waves.

She back paddled, rethinking her need to experience the wild river before it was tamed. There was a reason they called it wild. She hesitated too late. The pull was too strong. Even if she fought, she could not win against the strength of the river.

Her little kayak hung for a second on the lip of the rapids before plunging between two high waves. She paddled as hard as she could to give herself momentum when she crashed into the first wave. She didn't know how to aim her little boat in order to keep from capsizing.

One, two! One, two! One, two! She dipped her paddles into the water and pulled with all her might. The tip of her kayak dug into the water at the base of one of the waves.

A wall of water towered over her.

She was gonna die.

She ducked her head and screamed.

Chapter 19

JASON DIDN'T HAVE TIME IN his crazy schedule for a visit to the village, but he'd put it off long enough. He'd tried several times to get hold of Cassie, but she wasn't answering her phone. He'd been on site at the dam all morning anyway, doing some training for management, so he wasn't far. The way her village was tucked so deep in the valley, he decided to believe she wasn't getting his messages. Either that or she was ignoring him on purpose.

He pointed his Land Cruiser toward Babakondji.

Going straight from the project to the village took him down some roads he hadn't traveled up to now, past some villages he hadn't seen. These were all in the original flood zone. They'd been evacuated long ago.

Friday was decision day for the last five towns. A team of negotiators would fan out across the region to get people to make official choices between curtain number one, door number two, and box number three. There were no bad choices this time. The offers were generous, and from what he'd seen, everyone would be taking a big step up.

When he reached the well where Cassie had given her ridiculous soapbox speech, he tried to remember how to get to her house. She'd led him down narrow, twisting alleyways between houses built at odd angles to each other. He didn't even know if a road went to her place, though he did remember there being a road of sorts outside her wall. But how to get there?

He turned right, but that road skirted him past the outer edge of the village with no opportunity to enter. Back the other way, it was the same. There might be tire tracks leading in through narrow passages, but his vehicle was much too big to travel them without hitting something. He went back and parked near the well.

There were no adults fetching water, just a couple of preteen girls and a handful of children.

A little boy looked at him, wide-eyed, when he got out. The child had a round tummy and thin arms and legs.

"Hello," Jason said. "What's your name?" He reached out to shake the toddler's hand.

The tyke started to scream. He turned and ran away as fast as his thin legs would move him.

"Yovo?" said an older girl, maybe seven or eight, from her perch in the tree he'd stood under the other day. It was a low, wide tree, dripping with bowling-ball-sized fruit, like melons or gourds. She wore a red dress and a huge grin.

He walked over to the girl. "Hello," he said. "I'm looking for the other yovo. Cassie. Have you seen her?"

The girl covered her mouth and giggled.

He turned around and looked to see the other children. "Has anyone seen her? Cassie?"

They stared back like he was an alien, which he was, in a way.

"She's——" How could he say what he needed without any words? He pointed to his hair. "She has hair . . ." He pointed at the girl in the tree's red-orange dress.

A boy of six or seven grabbed his hand. "Yovo?" he said. "Good evening, good evening. Come."

He led Jason in the right direction. Jason started to recognize things he'd seen before.

At Cassie's house, the boy led Jason straight into the courtyard. The boy still held his hand. His fingers felt soft and damp.

Jason wasn't sure whether to knock. The boy showed no intention of leaving. "Hello?" Jason called, but got no answer. "Hello?"

A woman poked her head out the door on the other end of the row house. "Allo?" she called. "Gbo nye fa?"

Jason scratched his head. Did no one speak English around here? His Spanish minor wasn't helping much in West Africa. Of course, it hadn't helped in Lithuania either. And it wouldn't help at his next job in Nepal. "I'm sorry," he said. "I'm looking for Cassie. Do you know where she is?"

The woman stared at him.

"Cass-eee," he said, very slowly.

Her eyes brightened. She understood! "Not here," she said.

Now that they'd gotten the obvious out of the way, Jason tried a harder question. "Do you know where she is?"

The woman said a lot of words really fast.

Jason just stared at her and shrugged.

"Bodo," she said. She waved her hands like across the water, then mimed someone punting in a boat or raft.

"At the river?" He copied her action back to her.

She grinned.

The little boy let go of Jason's hand so he could pretend to swim through the air.

At the river. Perfect.

"When will she be back?" He tapped his wrist to ask for the time, but only got another blank stare. He pointed to the sun moving across the sky.

She shrugged and shook her head. She didn't know.

Jason took out a business card and scrawled a note to Cassie on the back.

There was nothing else he could do, so he headed back to the capital in plenty of time to make it home before dark.

Chapter 20

CASSIE DUCKED HER HEAD AND closed her eyes. She sliced into the wave as it crashed over her. Half the river forced itself up her nose and down her throat. She didn't even know she'd clenched her eyes shut until she opened them again. She gasped for air. Another wave loomed ahead. She paddled hard right, trying to steer herself to ride the side of this one instead of plowing straight through it. She wasn't strong enough to make the boat obey her. Instead of skirting sideways, she turned completely around. The river lifted the back of the kayak and smashed over her head. She held her breath, waiting in the darkening roar until the river sucked her out the other side of the wave.

Again, she paddled hard. The blade of her paddle hit against something. The Bodo wrenched the paddle from her hands.

She grabbed after it, but the paddle was gone. She mustn't panic, even though she had no way to control the boat. The kayak rode up the side of the next wave. Cassie tried to tip her body to keep upright, but the force of the water was too strong.

The little boat flipped. Time stopped. The world went black and then blue. Her heart beat inside her ears.

Time started again. She couldn't breathe. She panicked, desperate to find which way was up.

She twisted her body, but couldn't flip upright.

Darkness pushed in on her. The world thundered. She had to get her head out of the water.

The strap. Undo the strap.

She fumbled for it. Her lungs screamed for air. She had little time. She tried not to think about hitting her head on a rock.

Think, Cassie. Think.

She pulled on the strap. It didn't break free.

She pulled again, harder this time.

It snapped apart in her hands.

She kicked her legs and broke away from the boat.

She still didn't know which way was up. She swam with all her might, hoping for air, starving for it. Her lungs seared.

At last, she broke the surface of the water. Water rushed, louder than raging thunder. She gasped in a huge gulp of air and water. Foam swirled around her. Another wave loomed above. She caught a quick breath, just in time to be slammed under again.

At least now she knew which way was which. At least now she remembered that her life jacket would keep her afloat. Above the roar of the rapids, she gasped for breath. She wheezed with each intake, then coughed out the water in her lungs.

She told herself not to panic. The river would carry her to safety if she let it. But the logic didn't make sense, and her body fought to save itself.

The river roared in her ears. It spun her forward and backward. She tried to keep her toes on the surface, pointing downstream, but it was like trying to float in a washing machine.

Breathe, breathe, breathe, she told herself. Her breaths came fast and shallow, little gasps that did not fill her lungs or feed her brain.

Another wave crested over her. She pointed her toes into it until it broke. She resurfaced once again, but this time was different. The washing machine had finished its spin cycle. She bobbed on the surface of a flat, calm river. Her heart beat like mad. Her frantic breathing drowned the sound of the raging water above her.

She turned in a full circle, getting her bearings. The rapids were to the north, which oriented her to home. Just downstream, the river widened and pooled. Near the bank, she spotted her bright yellow kayak. No need to swim for it. It was caught in a dead place where the current did not reach. The Bodo would take her there.

She still gasped for each breath, but less now. As she floated, her breathing returned to normal. Her heartbeat slowed.

Wild hornbills whistled from the trees along the riverbanks.

Wild, she thought, not for the first time. Beyond the lust for electricity was the need to keep this small piece of Nkuve wild. The ETN wanted to harness the power of the river, but to harness it was to steal its freedom and everything that gave it the majesty it deserved.

She touched the side of the kayak with relief. The paddle floated nearby. The little boat seemed like a refuge. If only she could get back on top where she belonged. After three failed attempts to climb on, she struggled to pull it partway out of the water so she could hop on. Safely aboard, she pushed off into the river. After only a few minutes, she rounded a bend.

The new dam loomed ahead, a monstrous wall of concrete flanked by piles of rock, gravel, and mud from the farms they had peeled back to build it. It was hard to imagine this entire concrete cliff buried under water, but when the valley filled, most of the structure would disappear.

The sight of it made her want to spit. It wasn't just the dam. She got that there was a need for electricity. She got that it created jobs. But it completely discounted the needs, wants, and rights of the people losing their homes. The destruction wasn't in the rerouting of the river or the plan to produce more electricity. Heavens, with all the nights she'd spent without power at her place, the idea of having electricity that would come to her without interruption was like the stuff of pipe dreams and science fiction.

She had bigger questions. Who was going to be hurt? Who would be displaced? And how could she keep them from falling prey to empty promises like their countrymen upstream? More than ever, now that she had met the people of Ngorogo, she needed to fight for the people of Babakondji. More than ever, now that she'd met the river in all its fury, she understood what would be lost.

She rowed the kayak along the river's edge and nosed its tip onto the shore. The plastic boat tipped back and forth as she wormed her way out of it. She stood in water up to her knees.

Water. How had this precious, life-giving commodity become the enemy? Everyone in Babakondji and the rest of the valley depended on the rains to water their crops. Even now, the whole region held its collective breath waiting for the first rain to fall.

Water was life. How many times had the well run dry? How many seasons had she joined her neighbors in the endless slog to draw water from another well in another village? Hadn't she prayed for rain along with everyone else?

The tinny honk of a car horn pulled her back to the river. She looked up to see SJ waving at her from behind the wheel of his multicolored car. She gave a wave and stepped onto shore, pulling the kayak behind her.

SJ met her on the bank. "Where's your shoe?"

She looked down at her feet. Only one foot still had its Keen. She must have lost it in the rapids. "I don't know."

He picked up one end of the kayak and helped her carry it up to his car. "How was the trip?" he asked.

He had no idea how complicated his question was, what emotions it stirred in her.

"It was good. Rougher'n I expected." What else could she say?

They worked together to strap the boat on the roof of the car. A handful of children gathered to watch, giggling at the ridiculous yovos and their silly toys.

Cassie got into the car. This time she remembered not to reach for the seat belt. She waved good-bye to the kids. When SJ put the car in gear and pulled onto the main road, the children followed, laughing and screaming. They were so cute, so full of life. They didn't understand the danger of chasing cars. Just like they didn't understand the danger of the rising water. They would likely swim in the lake that was forming. Would they even remember their ancestral home?

She shook her head.

SJ glanced over at her. "What?" he asked.

"What what?"

"You shook your head."

She stared out the window. "There's just some things about this place I don't get. I don't think I ever will, even if I live here forever."

"Like what?"

"Like how parents pray so hard to have children, but don't bother protecting them from obvious danger."

"Obvious to who? Our idea of what makes something dangerous might not be the same as theirs."

She hit her fist on the dash. "Obvious to anyone. What about chasing cars? Playing with gunpowder? Catching, roasting, and eating mice?"

"They've just got a different way of looking at cause and effect. You're looking at it like a Westerner, as if there's a physical cause for everything. That's what makes us hypersensitive to safety. It's also what makes us so litigious."

Cassie squirmed. She didn't consider herself the suing type, but wasn't that the first place she went to look for ways to stop the dam? Tomorrow morning she'd be making plans with a lawyer to stop the ETN. She changed the subject. "I've never seen rapids like that before. I mean, I've been on float trips, but never on a wild river."

"They surprised me the first time, too. I can't get enough of them. I'll be sorry to see them go."

"I thought I was fixin' to drown at one point. But it was beautiful and majestic and amazing and powerful and something to be treasured and preserved, but they're gonna block it up and bury those rapids. I can't believe it'll all be gone."

He grunted. "Like Celilo Falls."

"Where?"

"Celilo Falls. It was this amazing set of rapids on the Columbia River near where I grew up. It was a traditional fishing grounds. I've seen pictures of men standing on wooden platforms over the falls, just scooping salmon out of the river. Before I was born, they built a dam downstream. It silenced the falls."

"What do you mean, silenced?"

"It flattened out the river, put the falls under the surface. Kind of a linchpin event in Oregon history."

"Yeah, but that was a long time ago. This is happening now."

"Not so long ago, really. My dad talks about fishing there. The falls were fifteen feet tall, and now they're gone."

"Like these will be." She couldn't imagine the rapids being erased. She couldn't imagine fifteen-foot falls just disappearing.

"All in the name of progress. Hydro power, recreation. Celilo was flooded to make navigation easier up the river. They say if you stand on the banks of the river and listen carefully, you can still hear them whisper."

She could almost hear them from here. "Have you heard them?"

"I've tried. It's like listening for a ghost. People who can hear it can hear a lot of other things I can't."

He seemed more saddened by the loss of these falls he'd never seen or heard than by the loss of this river that ran through his life right here and now.

"I've got to stop the same thing from happening to these rapids. Can you help?"

He shook his head. "It's too late."

"I can't believe that. At first, I was only trying to save Babakondji. I wanted to help my friends, my neighbors, but most of them have already given up. I don't get it."

"Why fight the inevitable?"

"Why does everyone assume it's inevitable? Or that it's not worth the trouble?" She sat silent for a minute. Ahead, a giant thunderhead towered like a cotton anvil above the thirsty land. That single cloud could hold the first rain of the year and the blessed coolness that followed. She hoped it would fall on Babakondji. Then she remembered it didn't matter. Their farms would be gone soon. The new land wasn't even divvied out, much less tilled. She said, "I've been thinking about Ngorogo."

"The dam?" SJ steered them toward the storm cloud. They would know soon whether it held any rain.

"No, the village. I talked to some people there this morning."

"And?"

"And the power company didn't keep its promises. None of them. People are worse off now than before the dam. It's sad to see, and it's what I was afraid of. There's no reason to believe things will turn out any better for my people."

"Maybe it's a different company. This one doesn't seem so bad. Our new village seems okay. We've been there a few months. It's not perfect, but it's okay. They've kept their promises so far. Why shouldn't I believe they'll keep the rest?"

"It's the same company. Enérgie Totale d'Nkuve."

"So maybe they changed their business practices since Ngorogo?"

You wish. "No way. They've got all the power. They can do whatever they want. We've got to stop them."

"We who?"

"Me and some friends. And whoever we can get to join us."

"Got any ideas?"

"I'm going to hire a lawyer, maybe play up the environmental angle."

"Sounds spendy. Any cheaper ideas?"

"Maybe a sit-in strike at the dam? They wouldn't let the floodwaters rush over us if we're sitting there."

SJ laughed.

"What's so funny?"

"Do you know anything about dams?"

"I know I don't like them, that they ruin people's lives and kill the habitats of innocent creatures."

He gave her a sideways glare. "It's great to be an idealist. I get that. I mean, why else would we join the Peace Corps? But you need to get your facts straight. You don't even know what you're up against."

What had she said?

"There's no floodwaters. They're filling a reservoir, not emptying it. It's like turning on the water in the bathtub. You could stage a sit-in, but all you'll get is raisiny toe wrinkles." He clicked his tongue like a local. "You're gonna need a different plan than that."

"Like what?"

"Not sure. But good luck."

"You're not going to help me? Take the next right. That's it."

"My visa's up for renewal."

Ah. No wonder he didn't want to get involved. No use riling the people who decided if you got to stay in their country.

They pulled up to her front door. The storm system was directly overhead now, shadowing the village and whipping it with strong wind. But no rain.

Cassie pulled her hair back in a ponytail before she got out of the car. She yelled through the open window. "Hey, thanks for the ride and the use of your boat."

"Anytime. If you want to borrow it again, I'm happy to loan it."

"I'll keep that in mind." She didn't think she could bear another trip down that river. One day was enough to make her fall in love with it. Another trip would only make things worse. She hung her head, disappointed by the lack of direction the trip gave her. Her friends had until Friday to decide what to do.

SJ started to pull away; then he stopped. He stuck his head out the window. "Hey, Cassie?"

"Yeah?" Despite her ponytail, hair lashed about her face. She raked it out of the way with one hand.

"I know a guy who knows someone who might be able to help out that village you were talking about. There's some farming methods that might help them get better crop yields. It's not much, but—"

"No, no. It's good. Thank you." It wasn't what she was hoping for, but it was better than nothing.

"And good luck with the lawyer."

She was gonna need it.

Chapter 21

OF ALL THE THINGS CASSIE ASPIRED to do in her life in Africa, hiring an attorney was not one of them. Yet here she was, outside the gate of one of the country's more prominent lawyers, praying for audience and answers. She hoped she'd have more luck meeting with him than with the absent PR guy at the dam. At least she had an appointment.

"Monsieur Antoine Viadji, Avocat" read the bronze plaque built into the white cement wall. A bougainvillea hedge drooped its raucous pink flowers over the top of the wall beside the metal gate, nearly obscuring the little sign.

Cassie pressed the doorbell next to the gate and listened carefully for a ringing from inside the house. She knew better than to assume just because there was a doorbell that it worked. She pressed the button again. This time she heard the distinct ding-dong of an old-fashioned chime.

She stepped back and waited. The gate wiggled a little. The clang and scratch of metal on metal lasted a few seconds. Someone on the inside opened a little window in the gate. An eyeball stared out at Cassie through a small rectangular opening.

Cassie gave a tentative smile. "I have an appointment?"

The eyeball backed away. The little window slammed shut. The latch of the big gate moved aside, and the gate swung open. A barrel-chested little man with khaki shorts and birdlike legs greeted her. "You are welcome," he said. "Please, follow me."

She minced her way up the drive, acutely aware that this house and all its amenities were like nothing she'd experienced in Nkuve before. Even the ambassador's house paled in comparison to this estate. The brick driveway was lined with marble squares. The box elder topiaries must be trimmed every morning.

She couldn't afford this guy. But he was the best, and she needed the best.

The waiting area of the lavish office also spoke of wealth. Most offices she'd been in since arriving in Nkuve were decorated with African art, wooden carvings or brightly painted scenes, often for sale. This room, though, was graced with pieces by, of all people, Matisse. She walked up to the one on the far wall, a blue-and-white print from his blue dancer series, but she'd never seen this one before. As she approached, she realized why. It wasn't a screen printing at all. It was an original. She pulled a card from her pocket to write down the name of the painting. It was the card Jason had left at her place. All it said was "Call me."

She hadn't.

"Mademoiselle?" A young woman in a bright green embroidered robe pulled her attention away from the painting. Her hair was done up in a head scarf that matched her robe in the local style that made Cassie think of royalty. "Mr. Viadji will see you now."

Cassie followed her through a pair of elaborately carved doors, down a marble-tiled hallway, into the attorney's office, a large room heavy with dark, weighty furniture that spoke the gravity of the office.

Mr. Viadji sat in a high-backed leather chair behind a massive mahogany desk. He knitted his fingers together. He was old enough to show a few gray hairs, young enough to use his looks to his advantage.

Cassie took a seat across the desk from him. She smiled what she hoped he would take as a friendly, confident smile.

He did not return the gesture. "How can I help you?" he asked. His white teeth exactly matched the collar of his starched shirt.

The leather chair was slippery against her cotton skirt. She gripped the front of the chair with both hands to keep from sliding around. "I'm from Babakondji." She took a breath, waiting for the name of the village to sink in, but he just stared back at her. "They're building a dam. It's fixin' to flood my village."

He didn't respond. It was going to be up to her to supply all the information he needed. She slid forward to the edge of the chair, as if grounding herself with both feet would give a solid base to the story she needed to tell.

"I am sure you have heard of the dam being built along the Bodo River. It's the second of three. It's been under construction for over a year, and those who are being involuntarily relocated were given warning and compensation months ago. Most of them, anyway. My village and four others were added to the impact zone in a recent recalculation of affected areas. We're being asked to evacuate, but are not being given time or recourse. Everyone else had a chance to speak out, but it's being denied us. Can you help?"

Mr. Viadji leaned forward to take a pen from a hand-carved pencil jar. He jotted something on a pad of paper. "Tell me about how you heard of the changes."

"It was in the paper. Can you believe it? They didn't even have the decency to tell us like humans. They just leaked the news to the press and let us find out by chance."

"And the reaction?"

"Panic. Chaos. Defeat. It depends who you talk to. For the most part, I'd say panic. Most of the village is subsistence farmers or women with small businesses. Very small. They don't have much education. They don't have the framework to see how this move will affect them."

Mr. Viadji clucked his tongue. "They are not stupid people."

"No, of course not." She didn't mean to give that impression at all. "They just don't have the experience to see how little they are being offered."

"And what is the offer?"

"Two point five million, give or take."

He jotted the number down, tapped his pen on the paper, then drew a circle around the number. "What is it you want me to do?" he asked. "Are you looking for help in negotiating a fair settlement? If so, there are other attorneys who are much less expensive who will take on cases for villagers. You may even find an NGO who would take this on pro bono."

Cheaper wasn't always better. "No, no, that's not what I want at all. I want to stop the dam, but I don't know how.

Do we have any recourse, any hope of stopping the project? You were the one who closed the phosphate mine."

"Those people were driven off their land with no offer of compensation. And the mine was stripping the land of any future usefulness."

"Our land will be under water. How useful is that?"

"But they are providing new houses, new farms."

She wanted to scream, but she composed her response. "In a place that is not their home—our home."

He tapped the pen on paper once more, then set it on the desk and leaned back. "I can look into its merits as a case, give you some ideas on which direction we could take, but I have to be honest with you. I'm not hopeful you would succeed. This is a government-backed project. The government has an interest in making sure it goes through. It does not sound like you are losing much by moving."

"I know we're paddling upriver, pardon the pun," she admitted. "If I didn't know that, I wouldn't need you. But I'm at a loss."

"Let me be clear up front. There is no guarantee I can do anything to stop this project. I can file injunctions and make a pest of myself. I can probably slow it, but perhaps not stop it. I charge for my time and for my staff's time. The hourly rate is three hundred thousand. We bill in six-minute increments. With no promises." He picked up the wooden pen from his desk blotter and scribbled some figures on a sheet of paper. "It's a rough guess, but my estimate is that in the first month of working on this, you would be looking in this neighborhood." He slid the paper across to her side of the desk.

It must be wrong. There was no way it could add up to that much. It was more than she'd been asking to fund projects for the whole village. More than it would take to fund the whole valley.

She blinked, half expecting the figure would change, that a zero or two or three would disappear.

They didn't.

"Do you want to proceed?"

She cleared her throat. "I'll have to think about it. I'll get back to you." She wouldn't. She'd have to find someone else, someone they could afford. Who was she kidding? She couldn't afford anyone. She lived in a rented one-room row house in the middle of nowhere in Africa, and her vehicle was a public taxi. She couldn't even afford to get her hair cut.

Once out on the sidewalk, Cassie allowed herself a minute of discouragement. She couldn't afford this lawyer. After only a minute of despair, she remembered she didn't have to fund it herself. She could get some backers.

Cam was definitely on the top of her list of people to call. He hadn't returned her message yet. She'd call him early, early tomorrow morning and try to catch him before he went to bed. Who else? There were a couple of embassy workers she had good rapport with. And then there was Jason. She tried him first. When he didn't pick up, she left him a message to call her back. She wished she could have gotten through to him or Cam or someone. But they'd call her back.

She had a good feeling about that.

Jason plopped down in his chair after lunch. The day's paper lay spread in front of him. Pierre from the *Ebésé* had written a fair article about the coming week's events. Nothing shocking from the opposition and, to his surprise, no quotes from a certain redhead.

Emanuel was the only one in the office today. The others had all been dispatched to the various communities to check on the building projects and manage negotiations with the residents. Jason wished he could be involved in this part of the process, but he'd found it best to leave the face-to-face talks to those who knew the culture and spoke the language. It was his job to get things rolling and to make sure the local task force was trained in how to do negotiations, not to butt his ugly American face into difficult conversations. In some places, people would resist cooperating because of his nationality. In others, they tended to do anything he suggested without regard to the impact on their own lives. Either way, these things were best handled without the complication of throwing a foreigner into the mix. He'd been there to make sure the offers were made according to plan. Now he just had to wait for fires to put out.

An icon blinked on his phone. He had a message. He pressed the button and listened as Cassie's voice came over the speaker.

"Hi, Jason. It's Cassie. I just spoke with a lawyer about the dam, a Mr. Viadji. I really want to hire him, but I and the whole village can't afford him. I'm thinking corporate sponsorship. Would your company be interested in financing some of the attorney fees? Call me."

Across the room, Emanuel whistled.

Jason looked at him. "What?"

"Is that who I think it is?"

"Yeah."

"She's trying to hire a lawyer, and she wants you to help her line up sponsors to pay him? Ha!" Emanuel slapped the desk.

Jason didn't think it was funny.

"It's ironic, don't you think?"

Ironic, yes. Funny, no.

"Wait. Did she say Viadji?"

"Yeah. I think so."

Emanuel whistled. "She does not mess around, does she?"

"What do you mean?"

"He is Nkuve's Johnnie Cochran. He is always in the middle of the big cases. And he is—how do you say it?—loaded. Not like rich-lawyer loaded but like dictator-of-a-small-country loaded. He wins every case."

Jason hadn't been worried until now. "Do you think he can beat us?"

Emanuel crossed his arms. "Every case."

If she could hire him. "If . . ." Jason had seen the projects she'd tried funding. She would never raise enough to hire this Viadji guy. Especially not if he was the one she was turning to for help.

He ought to call her back and tell her no. He *really* ought to call her to tell her *why* he had to say no. It was the kind of conversation you should have face to face. He wished he'd seen her when he went to her place yesterday. The note he'd left didn't tell her anything. He needed to talk to her in person.

Chapter 22

CASSIE WORRIED OVER THE COST of the attorney all the way home. She wished she'd been able to get through to Jason. Hopefully he'd call back soon. She didn't want to pin too much hope on him coming through for her. After all, he'd never really offered more than a sympathetic grunt as she'd spilled her heart about losing her home. But she knew he had resources, and she could tell he had a good heart. She was just giving him an opportunity to put them both to use.

She had another idea for a sponsor, one that might be even better, but Cam wouldn't be home from work in the States until the middle of the night local time. She would call him first thing in the morning.

After the taxi dropped her off, her feet took her to Elli's place, where she found her friend hauling everything out of her family's two-room house.

Cassie blurted out, "What's going on?"

Elli looked at her with a huge grin on her face. "We decided. We are taking a house in the new village."

She was too late. "You signed the papers?"

Elli shook her head. "This afternoon. We can move as soon as we want."

So, almost too late, but not quite. "They've already built the new village? When? How?" They'd only announced Babakondji was being flooded last week. They hadn't had time to excavate a new village, much less build houses in it.

Elli tipped her chin toward the west. "It's not far from here. Up the hill and down in the next valley."

"But there are no houses there. They'll need to build them."

Elli shrugged. "The first ones to sign will get the first houses." Elli grinned. "We will have electricity. In our house!"

"Wait." Cassie put her hands to her head. She couldn't think. "There's no village. There can't be. They haven't had time . . ."

"We could look." Elli set down the bundle of clothes she held. "It is not far. We should go?"

Cassie blinked. Well, why not? If Enérgie Totale d'Nkuve was getting unsuspecting people like Elli and her family to move out by promising them houses that might or might not exist, she'd love to get some evidence. "Bon." She checked her phone to make sure it had life left in case they ended up needing to take pictures for evidence. Plenty of juice. "Yeah, let's go."

She started out at a good clip, eager to prove to Elli that the village she'd been promised did not exist. She pulled ahead of Elli as they left Babakondji, eager to get there and prove her wrong. Within a few minutes, sweat soaked through her shirt. It ran into her eyes, stinging them with salt. She felt a little dizzy. She stopped to rest and turned to look behind her.

Elli was coming, taking one slow step after another in that maddening, unhurried pace of everyone here. She wasn't sweating at all. Elli's younger sister, Ablaga, walked beside her, carrying Fabrice on her back. A half-dozen other kids ran circles around them, stirring up dust into a cloud.

Cassie didn't cool off, but at least her stomach settled. She waited for Elli and the children to catch up with her. She pulled at the neck of her T-shirt to wipe her face. If she'd been patient in the first place, she might not have broken a sweat, but now that she'd opened those pores, there was no closing them.

Halfway up the hill, the children got distracted by a couple of lizards chasing each other. Cassie and Elli walked on, leaving the kids behind. Elli seemed, as always, at ease without having to fill the silence with conversation. For Cassie, leaving things unsaid made the meters stretch out before her. "I met an attorney today," she said.

"Oh?"

"He's got some ideas. I think he could help us. We just need to come up with the . . ." She realized she didn't know the local word for *retainer*. ". . . with the money to pay him." She also just now realized that the attorney would make more in one day than Elli and the others would be given for total compensation for leaving their homes. The distance between the rich and poor back in the States was nothing compared to here.

"How much?"

"A lot. I'm working on it."

They walked in silence but for the gentle slapping of flip-flops against the bottoms of their feet and the gentle rustling of palm fronds overhead. They crested the hill and started down into the valley. This one hung higher than the one they'd come from. The water would not reach this high.

A hundred yards or so down the hill, the dirt path widened. Just beyond, it became a paved road, wide enough for two cars as long as no one was walking or biking along it. A trench on either side showed the kind of foresight Cassie had come to not expect. What was going on here? How long had this been here? Someone had gone to the trouble of actually laying out a drainage plan before starting to build.

Ahead, a dozen houses stood in two straight lines, six on each side of the road. Not fancy, not big, but definitely complete and definitely new. They were built from cement blocks, painted with fresh whitewash, with red bars on windows and doors. Or rather, where the windows and doors would be installed. For now, the openings stood empty like yawning mouths and hollow eyes.

Two streetlights stood like tall, thin egrets.

"Nyawoa?" Elli said, her word of disbelief echoing Cassie's thoughts. "A real city."

Not nearly a city, but not a village either. "It looks like it."

On one side of the street, the houses were abuzz with workers feverishly cementing window frames in place. The houses on the other side sat silent. Cassie headed for the closest one. As she approached, she could see it was a duplex. So there were twenty-four units here, not quite enough to accommodate all those they were planning to displace from Babakondji, but more than she'd expected. The houses were conspicuously missing driveways. "Where are the—" She realized she didn't know the word for *driveway*, not in French or in Ewé. She hunted for another way to ask. "Where will people park their cars?"

Elli tilted her head. "What cars?"

Good point. No one in Babakondji had a car, so why would they need a driveway? She stepped across the drainage ditch into the patch of dirt that was more likely to become a family's cornfield than a front lawn. "Let's look inside."

Elli hesitated.

"Come on. No one is here. Don't you want to see what you'd be moving into?"

"Yes . . ."

"Then come on." She reached the front door in six steps. "Anyone home?" she called. As expected, no one answered. She pulled on the bars that blocked the doorway, and they swung open. She stepped inside.

The outside might look done, but the inside was still a construction site. Channels dug in the unpainted walls mapped where the electricity would run from an outlet to a light switch to a spot near the ceiling that would probably hold a long fluorescent lightbulb. It smelled of damp cement and whitewash. The packed dirt floor would get coated with a layer of pure cement so thin it would only look new until someone took the first step onto it and started a series of cracks that would never be repaired. The size and shape of the room, the high, small windows, reminded her more of a cell than a house.

"Is this it?" Elli asked from the doorway.

Cassie turned around. "It looks like there's another room." She stepped through the opening to the back half of the house. Straight ahead were two doorways. One of the tiny rooms was tiled on the floor and up the walls. The other was also tiled, with a hole in the middle of the floor. The builders had allowed for a bathing room and a squat toilet. On either side of these two rooms were two bedrooms, both tiny and spare. No closets, no kitchen. Surely they couldn't expect people to move their families into such a tiny space. Elli pressed up behind her to get a peek at the bedroom, if you could call it that.

Cassie, squeezed by the proximity of her friend and the closeness of her breath, fled outside. The open space helped her breathe better, but the memory of the small, dark space wouldn't leave. No one should have to live in these houses, if you could call them that.

"I love it," Elli said. She stood in the doorway, her face aglow with excitement.

Cassie stared at her. "You like it?" They'd been in the same house, seen the same things, yet had very, very different reactions. "There's not much to it."

"It is perfect," Elli said. "Or it will be once it is finished. Two bedrooms *and* a salon. It is like a mansion." She stepped outside and turned to look at the house. "Yes. We can be happy here."

Her world was too small.

Chapter 23

CASSIE WORRIED OVER WHAT TO DO. Her good friend and her family were ready to trade the village for a handful of magic beans, or as good as. Elli had it in her head that the replacement housing she was being offered would more than compensate for their loss. Cassie knew they deserved much more.

The next morning, as soon as it was light enough to sweep, Cassie climbed the hill. Again.

On her list of contacts, she found the avatar for Cam. He looked exactly the same, so much the same that she leaned in closer. It was the same, as in identical. It was their senior photo—him the football star, her the doting cheerleader. Only she had been cropped out of the photo, all but the tips of her fingers that wrapped around his side.

She couldn't do it, not after all these years, not after all that had happened.

No, she reminded herself. *It wasn't him. It was me. I was the one who walked away, who needed to explore the world.* He'd never dreamed of anything bigger than their small hometown in Arkansas or the mega company that was headquartered there. Bag boy, floor clerk, assistant manager, manager. He'd worked his way up the honest way and would keep climbing in the company until he was really somebody.

Somebody in corporate America. She chased away the what-ifs. She was living the life she wanted. *She* was making a difference. And now she had to come back to him, hat in hand, and ask for a piece of the success she'd rejected when she rejected him.

Hat in hand. It was no accident that the word in the local language for *please* literally translated "I take off my hat."

Now or never, she told herself. She pulled a crumpled sheet of paper from her breast pocket and flattened it on the ground next to her phone. These were her talking points, the most important items she needed to emphasize in order to gain his empathy for the cause. Which ones were most likely to reach him? Would he be motivated by the plight of the people of Babakondji? She doubted it. The faces and names of people here would be so abstract to him there. Even on her visits home, she was always shocked by how otherworldly her African life was. Just like her American life seemed like a dream when she was on this side of the ocean.

Would he be moved by the destruction of native landscapes? Not likely. He worked for a company, after all, that built an empire on the notion of taming the world and bending it to your will.

What about the impact on fish and wildlife? Again, it was a question for another place. He hadn't seen enough of the world to realize how much man's taming of the wild rivers hurt the creatures that lived there. She'd heard of the decline of salmon in America because of all the rivers being dammed. What impact would this dam have? She didn't even know. Were there any creatures that would decline or disappear because of this flooding? It was hard to imagine, but it had happened in other places many times before. What was the Nkuve equivalent of the silvery minnow, the tiny fish that used to swim the length of the Rio Grande? Now they were endangered, inhabiting only a narrow span of river between two dams. What were the silvery minnows of the Bodo? She had no idea. Honestly, she didn't know the river at all. She had rarely seen it, since it was not on the way to anywhere. If she did know what wildlife would be impacted by the dam, would Cam even care?

Probably not.

She let her eyes move down the list of arguments, and she talked herself out of every one. All but the last one, perhaps the weakest of all. *It means the world to me.*

Why should he care? He'd moved on with his life, settled down with his second choice—not in quality but in timing—Cassie's best friend, Teffany. Former best friend.

She took a deep breath. The air hung thick and hot. It was hard on days like this to even breathe in. It was winter back home, and though she hadn't checked the weather lately, she didn't need to. It was likely to be eighty degrees colder there than here.

She pressed the little video camera button and listened to the musical ring of the outgoing call.

Cameron's face appeared on the screen. It was night there, and he sat in the dim light of a living room, illuminated only by the blue light of a TV screen, or perhaps his computer screen. He looked more mature.

"Hi, Cass. Long time no see." He smiled, but it was hard to tell through the pixelated image whether he was happy to see her or not.

"Hi. How's things?"

"Good."

A wisp of blond hair darted past behind him, one of his little girls running by, no doubt.

"Who's with you?" Cassie asked.

"Oh, that's my little helper Annabelle. She's supposed to be in bed, but she seems to be busy with other things." He turned to look behind him. "Aren'tcha, squirt?"

The little girl disappeared from the screen, then reappeared in front of the couch, squirming into her daddy's lap.

Cassie's heart tightened a little. That little girl should have—no, could have—been theirs. The whole package, really, the suede couch, the pendulum lights, the big-screen TV, and the fancy cars. Even the white picket fence. But that's not the life she'd chosen for herself. It wasn't where she belonged.

"She's gorgeous, Cam. You're so lucky. How old are you now, sweetie?"

The little girl stared at her for a minute, then carefully held up two fingers. A third one wanted to pop up, but she dutifully held it down.

"Two? You're so big." Her heart wanted to burst with the beauty, the promise of this child. She thought of Fabrice, whose future was less certain.

Annabelle scrambled off her daddy's lap and disappeared.

"How is Teffy?"

Cam turned his head away from the camera. "She's asking about you, hon. Come say hi."

Cassie heard a voice, muffled, from the other room.

Cam turned back to her. "I guess she's up to her elbows in dishes. She says hi."

Sure she did. Teffy hadn't spoken to Cassie since saying yes to Cam's proposal. It took a long time for Cassie to want to talk to her, but she was over that now.

The screen froze, and Cam's face turned all pixelly.

Cassie waited for it to clear up. She needed to go ahead and ask before she lost her nerve or the call got dropped. As soon as his voice caught up with his picture, she started in.

"Hey, Cam, this isn't just a social call."

He leaned in. "I figured."

"They're damming my village."

"You mean condemning?"

"No. Well, yes. They're building a dam across the river near where I live. They've already relocated a bunch of people in other villages, but they miscalculated. They're going to flood the village where I live if we don't do something about it."

"Like what?"

The sting of unbidden tears made her blink. "I don't know. I've worked on a bushel of projects, but saving a town isn't in my repertoire. I want to hire an attorney."

"Ah. And that's where I come in?"

"Exactly. You'd be helping save the homes of hundreds of people. These are people who are living on a dollar a day. Losing their homes will be devastating."

"What's the name of the project?"

"The Central Bodo Hydroelectric Project."

He wrote it down. "And you've talked to an attorney there?"

She gave him Viadji's name and cost. He didn't bat an eye when she told him the hourly rate. That could be a good sign.

"Listen, Cass, I'm obviously not going to say yes or no right now. I need to look into it, see what the project timelines look like, what protests have already been filed. I'll have to talk to Teff about it, too. Can we plan to talk in a few days?"

A few days would be too late. "We have two days. If you can make it sooner . . ."

He stuck his pen behind his ear. "Two days until the flooding? That's cutting it pretty close."

"Until they need to make a decision. Ten until the flooding."

"Still pretty quick. If I have to decide without all the facts, the answer is usually no. Give me the time I need to make an informed decision, and I'll give you an honest answer about whether I think I can help or not. I'll try to be quick. Is that fair?"

"Fair enough." What choice did she have?

Cassie's calls to her expat friends were no more productive than to Jason and Cam. Even though she didn't have the funding secured, Cassie needed to get the ball rolling with Mr. Viadji so he would have time to file something—anything—in time to stop the flooding. Something would surely come through.

She dialed the lawyer's number. A secretary answered.

"I'd like to speak to Mr. Viadji, please?"

"Concerning?"

"This is Cassandra Perth. I spoke to him yesterday about the Central Bodo Project. I told him I'd let him know as soon as possible if I was going to retain his services."

"Miss Perth, you said?" It must be the voice of the elaborately dressed woman who had escorted her into the office.

"Yes."

"Hold on, please."

A synthesized track of hold music played in her ear. Cassie practiced what she would say when Viadji came on. She had to convince him that even though she didn't have the money in hand, she was ready to go forward with their plan. After a few false starts, she thought she found exactly what she wanted to say.

She was expecting Mr. Viadji to come on the line, but was surprised by the secretary's voice. "Miss Perth? I'm sorry, but Mr. Viadji is unavailable to speak with you at this time."

Cassie swallowed her prepared statement. "Wh—when will he be able to talk?"

"Not soon, I'm afraid. He's recently been retained by the IMAN Group. You can give his name to your own attorney."

The IMAN Group? Wasn't that the name of the PR firm that was supposed to smooth things over in the villages? "But—" *He is my attorney*, she wanted to say, but all that came out was "Oh."

"Have a nice day, Miss Perth."

It took Cassie a second to react. "Wait—the IMAN Group?" It couldn't be a coincidence.

"That's right."

But how did they know? And why would they need a lawyer besides the ones they already had? "Can you tell me who from that firm communicated with your office?"

"I'm sorry."

This time she hung up before Cassie could think of a retort.

Cassie sank to the ground.

Sabotage was the word that echoed in her head.

Chapter 24

CASSIE TRUDGED BACK TO Babakondji. She still had people to call to help with funding, but with her attorney snatched out of her grasp, she didn't know what she'd be raising money for. She needed to regroup.

At home, Koffi was working in the common courtyard. He had spread an avo across the ground in a wide rectangle. He pulled a shirt off the clothesline, folded it, and placed it in the center of the cloth.

It was one of Cassie's shirts. Why was her shoe-making neighbor folding her clothes?

"What are you doing?" Cassie asked.

"Packing your things."

"I'm not going anywhere." Cassie leaned over and picked up the shirt, flicked it open, and started to hang it back on the line.

Koffi took the shirt back and tossed it on the avo without folding it. "We're all going somewhere." His gaze did not meet Cassie's. Not a good sign.

"What happened?" Cassie asked.

"I got a job."

"Doing what?" As far as she knew, Koffi's only skill was repairing leather shoes. He didn't have an education. He couldn't even read.

"Night watchman for one of the managers at the cité. It's a good job, steady pay, and it comes with a boyerie."

Cassie cringed at the word for an extra apartment in the compound, but that brought to her mind images of racist redneck relatives who didn't see anything wrong with calling a grown black man "boy." Koffi probably didn't even know where the word came from, but Cassie did and she hated it.

"I thought you were going to help with the strike."

"I would have, but this job pays more than I've ever made before."

Sounded too good to be real. "What if they're just offering you the job now to get you out of your house, and as soon as they get you moved, they fire you?"

Koffi stopped folding the towel he had in his hands and stared at Cassie like she was a crazy woman. "Why would they do that? I am a hard worker. I will stay awake."

She knew it sounded crazy, but she'd met those people in Ngorogo and heard what had been promised them and what they actually got. "I don't know why. I just . . . I don't trust them. I'm worried about you is all. I want Babakondji to still be here a year from now, ten years from now, and long beyond that."

Antoinette, the landlord, stepped out her door on the far end of the row house. She was wrapped in an old avo. She stretched and yawned, one of those loud yawns that alerted everyone she was around. She ambled over to Cassie and Koffi. "What's happening?"

"I got a job." One corner of Koffi's mouth turned up. He puffed out his chest full of tiny curlicues of black hair.

Antoinette scratched her back. "Good for you."

Koffi resumed folding the towel. "What about you? What are your plans?"

"I'll take the settlement, of course. They're compensating me for all my properties, so it will be a nice amount. I can invest it elsewhere."

Cassie spoke up. "We have a saying in America."

Antoinette raised one eyebrow. "You have many, as I recall."

She was referring to how, in Cassie's first years here, she brought up American thought, American customs, American food, American life in every conversation. It was a normal part of adjusting to a new culture. That was before Cassie had heard another volunteer do the same thing and realized how obnoxious it sounded.

"What is your saying?" Koffi asked.

Cassie couldn't translate it exactly, so she came as close as she could. "If you have a bird in your hand, it is worth more than two birds in the woods."

Koffi and Antoinette both stared at her. Proverbs and sayings didn't always translate well, but this one should be obvious.

She rephrased. "It's better to keep what you have than to give it up on the chance of something better. You might end up with nothing."

Koffi squinted. "But sometimes you must let go or you will have no chance for something better."

"But not this time." Cassie knew she sounded like a spoiled child, but they didn't realize how things were sure to turn out.

Koffi put his fists on his hips. "Why can't you be happy for me?"

"I am. I'm not mad. I'm just—I don't trust the power company. I think they mean to trick you out of your land and homes."

"Why would you think that? They made a mistake, but they have worked hard to correct it."

"I just came from Ngorogo. I saw what their life is like."

Antoinette asked, "What did you see?"

"They were promised the same as you if they would leave—jobs, houses, money, and restitution for lost crops. They didn't get any of it."

"They did not build them houses? Then it is not the same. They have already started building ours. Have you seen?"

"No, yes. They did build houses, but they're crummy. Crumbly. They're falling down. They were given land, but it's no good. It's dead land. They can't grow anything. The money they were promised stopped as soon as the village was under water."

Antoinette's eyes widened in panic. "Is it true?" Not that it should matter to her. She was leaving anyway.

Koffi put his hand out to quiet her. "Of course not."

"Is what true?" It was Niko. He and Elli arrived together.

Cassie stepped back a little to welcome them into the conversation.

Koffi said, "The yovo thinks the ETN is making promises they will not keep. She says we will end with no jobs, no houses, no money if we agree to their terms."

"It is the same we will end with if we do not agree," Elli said. "What else can we do?"

Niko said, "There is nothing to do. We are not Ngorogo. This is not happening here. My fofo lives in one of the other villages they relocated, not far from here, and he is already in a new house, larger and better than his old one. It is made of cement."

Cassie shook her head. "A little cement and a bushel of sand. His house will not last."

Koffi shook his head back. "That's not how these people are. They are being very generous."

"Generous or deceitful? Don't believe anything they tell you. Imagine the worst and then imagine worse than that. They are snakes."

Koffi said, "Would a snake feed its prey? They've already offered us more jobs than any of the villages that were in the original flood zone. The numbers are good. They are already sending the money they promised people to their phones."

"Full payments?"

Niko piped in. "Not yet, but the first installment. Look." He handed Cassie his phone and showed her how much money had already been transferred. Not a lot, but to someone who had never had a paycheck in his life, it must seem like he'd won the lotto.

"I know what it looks like," Cassie said. She hardened her tone and spoke to each of them in turn, directly looking into their eyes to impress on them the seriousness of her words. "They're giving you money. They're promising you jobs. But I'm telling you . . . I understand these people. They're not even people, really, just parts of a machine. And they're willing to do anything and say anything to get you out of their way. Their promises are a lie."

Niko shook his head. "How can you be sure?"

"They're just trying to move you out of their way. How long have we known each other? Don't you trust me by now?"

"Yes, but . . ." He held out his phone. "It's real money."

"It's blood money," Cassie said. "Please, Niko, stand with me. Koffi, you too. It is for your own good."

Koffi said, "What can we accomplish? It is too late to stop them."

At last, a glimmer of hope for help. Cassie grabbed on to it with earnest abandon. "It's never too late. At least we can try."

Niko looked at his phone again. "Do we have to give the money back?"

"Not now. Not unless it works. And then you won't need the money because you will still have your homes."

Niko looked at her skeptically. "It's a lot of money."

It was less than fifty dollars. Again, relative.

"Look," Cassie said. She pulled out her phone and pulled up the photos she had taken at Ngorogo. "Here is what the houses look like."

The other gathered around to see the little screen.

Niko whistled. "How old is that house?"

Cassie said, "As old as the dam. Eight years at most." She swiped the screen. "And here is the land."

"Ooo," Koffi moaned. "Menyo."

"Not good at all," Cassie agreed, though she didn't see it with full understanding like he did.

"But what can we do?"

Finally! Cassie leaned in with her plan. "Have you ever heard of a peaceful protest?"

"Like Gandhi?" Niko asked.

"Yes, exactly!"

Elli asked, "Who is Gandhi?"

Niko explained, "He was a very small man with very big ideas. He taught people to fight by not fighting."

Elli scrunched her face. "How is that possible?"

Niko searched for a way to explain. "He taught them that they could fight the government by refusing to buy clothes from the West, by making their own salt, by refusing to eat."

"Nyawoa?" Elli asked Cassie. "Is that your idea? Are we going to make salt and stop eating?"

She laughed. She was sure any one of them could outlast her in a hunger strike. She couldn't even make it to lunchtime without eating. "That's the idea, but we're not protesting British rule through control of salt and cotton. We're protesting for the right to live in our own homes."

Kofi asked, "How?

"I was thinking of a sit-down strike, but I don't think that will work. So I have another idea. We're going to need some paint—actually, a lot of it—rope, and dark clothing for everyone. Who's in?"

Chapter 25

THE WAY KOFFI CLICKED HIS tongue, Cassie could tell he had a reason he didn't want to join the protest. "What is it?" she asked. "I know you don't think it will work."

He shook his head. "It's dangerous."

"We'll spot each other. We'll be careful."

"Not the actual protest. I mean, it could be dangerous, but that's not what I'm worried about."

"What, then?"

"Protests in general. You weren't here, but we remember. Twenty years ago, there were countrywide strikes for higher wages. By the time the police finished shooting anyone who was protesting, we were happy to just be alive, never mind having work or not. It took us years—years—to recover. Those who were indicted for protesting were arrested on all kinds of trumped-up charges. Some were executed, some thrown in prison and forgotten."

"That was a long time ago. This is a free country."

"Freedom has many meanings."

Cassie knew there was corruption running through all levels of government, but she couldn't believe it would spill out in violence over something as small as graffiti. "Things like that don't happen now."

"We may wear the skin of civility, but our thirst for power lies just beneath the surface."

Niko piped in. "He's right. I was a child. My uncle was killed in those protests."

Koffi added, "And worse than the killing—no offense to your family—was the hunger that followed. There was no work for anyone."

"When he says years, he's not exaggerating." Elli had been so quiet up to now. "I even remember that, and I wasn't born until after the strikes. Papa used to have a steady job as a teacher. After he participated in the strikes, he was never able to get a teaching job again. That's why we moved back to the village, so he could farm the family land."

Cassie had no idea that Elli's father was educated. She'd always assumed he was a farmer because he didn't know how to do anything else.

"Come on, guys. It's just one night. We go and leave our mark, and then we're done. If it doesn't work, we give in. I promise."

Niko shook his head. "It's over for you, but not for us. The worst that happens to you is that they send you to America. I'd do anything for that kind of punishment. But what if I get caught? What then?"

"It's not a felony. At worst it would be considered vandalism. They slap our hands and let us go."

"No, they let you go. Us, they hold. It's different for you."

"Equal punishment for equal crimes. We get punished or rewarded the same."

Koffi laughed. "Where do you come from?"

"What?"

"You don't see how you are treated differently? Look at you. You are American. Not to mention you are white. Very, very white."

"Oh really? You think I hadn't noticed? I get screamed at everywhere I go because of the color of my skin. It's no great honor."

"Why are you even picking this fight?" Koffi asked. He might be the one to say it, but no one else jumped in to challenge his question. Not even Elli.

Now her hackles were up. "Why do you think? Everything I own is in that little room. I've lived here all my adult life. Babakondji is my home, just like it is yours." How many times did she have to have this conversation before someone believed her?

"If Nkuve falls into strikes or wars or famine, will you still be here? If you catch typhoid or AIDS or Ebola? You Americans get airlifted to a special hospital by a special plane. We are left here to die. Wherever you escape to, that's your home. There is no rescue for us. That's the difference."

She had wrestled with these questions over and over. She liked to think she was strong enough to stay, no matter what. "If I get caught, they could kick me out of the country." Against her will, a tear slipped out of the corner of her eye. She swiped it away before they could take it as a sign of weakness.

While Antoinette patted her shoulder and said "Evo" over and over, Koffi, Elli, and Niko stuck their heads together and discussed the situation. They rattled off one argument after another, but Cassie couldn't follow their reasoning. Her knowledge of the local language was good, but not good enough to follow rapid-fire discussion. At least they were discussing it now. A few minutes ago, they were blowing her off.

They brought up some good points. The punishment for an act of vandalism in Nkuve was much harsher than where she grew up. Kids in her hometown used to tag walls all the time. Mostly they didn't get caught, but if they did, they were given a bucket and towel and told to clean it off.

Obviously there were things about a place you didn't know if you didn't grow up there. She'd heard stories that during World War II, a way to find out if someone was a spy was to ask them to supply the next line of a nursery rhyme.

Peter, Peter, pumpkin eater had a wife and couldn't keep her . . .

Little Miss Muffet sat on her tuffet eating her curds and whey . . .

Three blind mice, see how they run . . .

Little pieces of information, little stories, hardwired into us as children, that you would never think to learn if you went to a new place. It's why she often felt left out of jokes here. She could understand all the words her friends were saying, but she couldn't grasp the humor. Still, she laughed along.

Punishment must be the same way. She knew not to blast through a police checkpoint. The soldiers with machine guns draped around their necks like bulky necklaces were enough of a reminder for that. Other than that, she knew the law said you had to keep your animals penned up. This one always made her laugh. She suspected it was a law put in place by car owners so they couldn't be blamed when they ran over a chicken or sheep or goat or cow.

They had debtor's prison here. That was different. But what else? Was there a punishment for ruining someone's property? Or, like most things, would it be handled by the village chief and his council? If so, she was golden. After all, the chief had already abandoned them.

The three drew apart.

Koffi looked at her. "Okay," he said. "We'll do it. But if it doesn't work, we are finished."

"You go ahead," Antoinette said. "I'm much too old to take such chances."

Cassie threw her arms around Elli's neck. She would have hugged Koffi and Niko, too, but stopped herself in time. "Thank you, thank you, thank you! It will work. I know it will."

Finally, things were going to go her way.

Cassie scribbled her ideas out in a flimsy composition book on loosely woven paper like the oatmeal-colored penmanship paper she'd used in elementary school, only not as good quality. It was a humble scratch pad for such a lofty project, a fifty-foot-tall poster across the face of the dam.

She drew a dotted line down the side of the page and sketched a pair of scissors cutting through it. She'd seen a photo of a dam with this design on it, an act of protest or ecoterrorism or however you wanted to name it, depending on which side you were on.

She turned the page. Too ambitious. Too exact. If she and her motley crew tried to draw a straight dotted line down the face of the dam, they would probably get caught halfway down. They didn't exactly have professional climbing gear. This would be a low-tech operation.

She thought about a big circle with a slash through it, but the symbol might not translate.

Bombs and guns and tanks were too violent.

Flowers and trees and houses too tame.

She wrote out a few words, but she wanted something that would mean something to those who spoke the native language. It also needed to be something that spoke to her own heart in the fight.

Stop/Noté.

I refuse/Me gbe.

Save our homes/De miafe homewo.

Too long. She tapped her pencil on the paper and stared at the last sentence. That was it! *Home* in English was most closely translated as "home," pronounced *hoe-may*, in the local language. It was a word that captured the heart of the struggle for all of them.

Simple, short, but they could paint it big enough to make a statement. Even if they couldn't win, they would go down swinging.

Chapter 26

THE FOUR OF THEM MET THAT night at the edge of the village. It had taken them a while to figure out transportation—none of them had a car, and they didn't want to take all their equipment in a taxi—but Niko had a fofo who had an old sedan that ran well enough to get them up the hill and down the valley.

None of them spoke on the ride to the dam, as if they already had to keep the silence that would keep them safe. In the car, Cassie sent a text to Pierre.

Take a picture of the dam in the morning.

She composed another to Jason.

Making a statement at the dam tonight. Wish me luck.

This wasn't his fight. Still, she needed to feel like someone out there was on her side.

Her note was cryptic enough he wouldn't have any idea that her statement would be literally painted on the dam, but on point enough for him to know she was making a move.

The temporary river was, to Cassie's surprise, dried up. All the water would build up behind the dam from now on. In the inky darkness, the stars reflected their light against the black water rising behind the dam. Since her kayaking trip, the pond had grown at least twenty times larger.

Koffi, Elli, and Niko climbed out of the car. Cassie was the last one out. She closed the door gently, holding on to it most of the way before easing it shut with a final soft click. Even the faint sound seemed to echo off the hills. She put her finger to her lips, a reminder to all of them to stay quiet.

She could feel the others' nerves even without seeing their faces. If they had the chance to look into each others' eyes, she didn't think she could go through with their plan.

They didn't know what kind of security to expect. She hadn't seen any dogs in the daylight. She could only hope there wouldn't be any at night. A patrol guard slumped down in a plastic chair, sound asleep.

She waved the others past him. If he was the only guard on duty, they had nothing to worry about. He could enjoy his night's rest.

They snuck across the parking lot to the edge of the dam. Cassie found another reason to be glad for the darkness. At least she couldn't see how far down it was. Since her last visit here, they had completed the top of the dam. Handrails lined both sides of a narrow sidewalk across the top. She tested the rails. They seemed sturdy enough. Still, she didn't trust them completely. Despite her fear of heights, she and Niko had agreed they would be the ones to do the painting while the other two controlled the ropes and passed down supplies as needed. It was only fair that she accept the risk, since it was her idea.

She was hoping to paint the letters at least fifteen feet tall, maybe more, depending on how long it took to actually lay down the paint.

They crossed the top of the dam as stealthily as they could. To begin, Cassie would do the *E* and Niko the *M*. When they finished those letters, they would move left and complete the word. As long as no one was on patrol, they could take all night. But without knowing what to expect, they would work as quickly as possible. The idea was to make a statement, not to get an art award.

"You lower me down until I hiss," Cassie said to Elli. "Gently, though. I don't want you to drop me."

Her friend stared at her with wide eyes, the whites showing all the way around her dark irises. "What do I do if someone comes?"

"Tie me off when I'm at the top of the letter. Here"— she pointed to the lower rail—"so they're less likely to notice. Then just duck down."

"But if someone crosses the dam—"

"Then we're sunk. Run if you want. I won't blame you. We'll hurry." She stepped into the handmade harness and pulled it to the top of her thighs. Already the ropes cut into her, and she wasn't even resting her weight on them yet.

She climbed over the railing. "You got me?"

Elli gripped the rope with both hands. Cassie hoped she was strong enough to hold her until she got down the side. She knew there was a right way to prep a rope for rappelling, and this wasn't it. Not even close. But she was limited to the resources available in Babakondji and the group's experience.

This was the best they could do.

With eyes closed and a prayer, she stepped backward over the edge.

Chapter 27

THE ROPE HARNESS CUT INTO the backs of her thighs. Her weight pulled the harness tighter around her waist. Above, she heard Elli groaning. She was going to have to work fast. Like really fast.

"Wrap it around the rail," she hissed. "It will help you hold me better."

Above, she heard Elli fussing with the rope, arguing with it to make it obey. She had to trust Elli would figure it out.

She gripped the rope with one hand, afraid she would flip sideways or—worse—upside down if she let go. In the other hand she held the bucket of paint with a giant paintbrush. The bigger the brush, the faster the job.

When she got down far enough to start the top of the *E*, she hissed. Her friend above stopped lowering her. She heard her messing with the knot. Cassie blocked it out of her mind. She could not—would not—allow herself to imagine falling. It was a worthy cause, but not worth dying for. Funny how the thought hadn't occurred to her until now.

She pulled out the huge paintbrush, more of a short-handled mop, really, and made her first mark. A straight horizontal line from as far as she could reach left to as far as she could reach right. That made it about five feet long. It would need to be much longer. And thicker.

She thickened the line, passing over it time and again, until it met her standards. Another hiss told Elli it was time to move. Cassie looked up. Her headlamp washed across Elli's face peering over the edge, looking at least as terrified as Cassie felt.

Cassie tipped her head to the right, indicating with her headlamp which way to move her.

Elli jerked on the rope, presumably freeing her from that section of handrail in order to move her down.

After she finished painting the other end of the *E*'s top leg, Cassie hissed again.

Elli's head appeared over the edge. She stage whispered, "Do you want to move over or down?"

Cassie glanced back at her work. Ten feet wide. That would make it fifteen feet tall. This was taking longer than she wanted. "Across," she said. It would take longer, but it would make a bigger statement. "You okay with that?" She looked over at Niko. He looked like he was struggling. An *M* was probably harder than an *E*. But ten feet wasn't enough.

By the time she finished the top line, her legs were asleep. And cramped.

Elli lowered her a few feet.

Cassie swung her arm up and down, painting messy, thick swaths of green on the light gray cement. In the dark, it appeared black on white. It didn't look like much now, but in the morning . . . she hoped it would draw the attention of the surrounding villages, the officials, the press. She wanted to go out with a bang. Or not go out at all.

She finished the top half of the upright, then the middle horizontal line. It wasn't quite even with the top one, but it'd have to do. It's not like she brought an enormous eraser with her.

"Sssst! Down again." She couldn't wait to finish this letter. One more line and she could get pulled back up to replenish her paint supply and move her legs around. Her feet braced her against the wall, but she couldn't feel them anymore. It reminded her of the pain of squashing her toes into too-small ski boots.

Elli slackened the rope, moving her down slowly with a groan.

And then, a yelp.

Cassie plummeted. She twisted, and her back scraped against the cement as she fell.

She was about to die.

She jerked to a stop. Her back pressed against the dam. She felt like she'd fallen a thousand feet. She scrambled around like a cockroach righting itself and braced her feet against the vertical again. Looking at the paint, she saw she'd only fallen about three feet. Far too much, by her count, but not enough to do any damage other than to her heart.

"You okay?"

She waved the paintbrush above her head. "I will be."

She set to work again, brushing out the last line like her life depended on it, which, in a way, it did.

Niko finished the M before she finished her E. With a thumbs-up, he got raised out of sight. Overhead, she heard some scuffling. It must be harder to get over the edge than she anticipated. Likely his feet were asleep, too.

More than anything, she wanted to stand up and shake some life back into her limbs.

At last, she finished the last line. She hissed for Elli to pull her up.

Nothing happened.

She hissed again.

The rope jerked, and she started the slow ascent up the sheer face of the dam. She wrapped her free arm around the rope, twisted around, and stretched out a finger to click off her headlamp. She didn't want the light appearing over the top of the dam to shine in the wrong direction and give them away. Slow and steady, she walked her feet up the wall, keeping up with the speed of the rope.

Finally, she reached the ledge. She swung her paint bucket and brush onto the level surface to free her hand.

A gloved hand reached down to help her.

Elli didn't have gloves.

She grasped the hand and pulled herself against it, swung her right foot up, and clambered on top. The rope loosened around her thighs. Blood rushed back into her limbs, giving her if not feeling, at least the hope of it. She ducked under the guardrail and stood to her full height.

She turned around to help Elli untangle the rope and found herself face to face with Jason instead.

Chapter 28

JASON?

At first she couldn't even react. Where was Elli? Or Niko and Koffi?

She looked around. Her three friends were gone.

"What are you doing here?" She gave him a side hug. "You didn't have to come, but I'm glad you did."

"Actually, I did have to come," he said. He pulled away. He wasn't smiling. He wore something around his neck, a lanyard with some kind of name tag.

It took a minute for her to realize. His name tag had the power company's logo on it. She felt like he'd punched her in the gut.

"But—you're—? What are you doing here?"

"I work here."

"You—" No. That wasn't right. It couldn't be. This was the company he worked for? This was the business she had imagined would help her fight the power company?

She put her hand to her mouth. She didn't feel so good.

"Come on." He grabbed her elbow and nudged her west across the top of the dam. On the upstream side, the moon's reflection danced across the gathering water, mocking her. She could be deported over what she'd done.

"Where are we going? Are you turning me in? Where are my friends?"

He squeezed her arm a little harder. "Just be quiet for a minute, will you? We don't want to wake the guards."

"We don't?" She wanted to turn to catch his expression, but he kept forcing her forward.

He marched her to the end of the dam and across the temporary parking lot. Even since they'd arrived, the water had risen. By morning, the lot would be covered.

At the edge of the lot, he stopped. He jerked on her elbow to turn her around, not hard enough to hurt, but enough she knew he meant business.

"What do you think you're doing?" he hissed.

She shook her elbow out of his grasp. "How could you not tell me?"

"You never asked."

She wanted to spit at him. "That's the stupidest, lowest—of course I didn't. Why would I think to ask? It should've come up."

"You wanted someone to listen to you. I listened."

"And offered advice. Biased advice, I might add. What did you do with my friends?"

"They're lucky, you know. I could press charges. Against you, too."

She was so mad, she didn't care. "You tricked me."

He shrugged. "If you recall, I tried to talk you out of it. You insisted."

"You could have told me I was in bed with the enemy."

"I don't remember getting in bed together."

She stomped her foot. "You know what I mean. If you'd said, 'By the way, I work at the dam,' I obviously wouldn't have come to you for advice."

"Obviously," he said. "I know you don't believe me, but I tried telling you. I didn't think you were going to do something this stupid. I can't imagine the jails around here are very nice."

Jail anywhere seemed like a bad idea, but he was right. She'd die in an Nkuvian jail.

"Are the police coming? Are they already here?"

He fished something out of his pocket and held it out.

A handkerchief.

"What's that for?"

"Wipe your face. The sooty look isn't doing anything for you. And I think you have some paint there." He pointed at the side of her nose. "And there," he said, waving his open hand all around.

She wiped at her face, as if she could remove the paint or the guilt of what she'd done. Only she didn't feel guilty, just mad that she'd been caught, that her friends had been taken away, that she'd made things worse than ever with nothing to show for it.

And most of all, mad at Jason for all the lies, all the deceit and the backstabbing. She wished the police would get here and take her away so she didn't have to talk to him anymore.

"I'll see you tomorrow," Jason said. He took a step away from her.

He wasn't going to wait for the police to get there? "Wait. Where are you going?"

"It's late. Go home. I'll pick you up at eight."

"What for?"

"To start cleaning up this mess."

"No police?"

"Put things back how they were, and we'll call it good."

Back how things were was better than jail, but worse than things were if it meant she had to help with erasing the damage. "There's no way."

He stepped back toward her. "You and your friends could be in a lot of trouble. A lot. Eight o'clock, or I press charges against all four of you."

She shook her head. "Leave them out of it. It's not their fight."

"I thought you were fighting for their homes."

"I am. I was. But they're not. They're just here because of me. Let them go. Press charges against me, whatever you want, but leave them alone."

"Tomorrow at eight. Dress for hard, hot work. I hope that paint is water soluble."

She hadn't even thought to check.

Cassie found her friends at the car, petrified. They rode back to Babakondji in silence. Cassie's mind ran a million miles an hour. She wanted to apologize, but didn't know how. She had no right to expect anything more from them.

It was time to let them go.

Chapter 29

ONCE CASSIE AND HER FRIENDS pulled safely away, Jason climbed behind the wheel of his Land Cruiser. He flipped on his brights and turned to the south. To his surprise, his hands shook against the wheel. He took deep breaths, trying to calm down.

It was a miracle the four vandals hadn't hurt themselves. Harnesses hand tied from rope, no helmets, no carabiners or safety lines—they were lucky they weren't dead.

He was lucky they weren't dead. He'd dealt with a bunch of crazy things in his different posts, but Cassie surprised him. He knew she had the passion, he just didn't think she had the gumption to follow through on it. Well, he was wrong.

He didn't get it. What was so bad about the dam? Her friends would be better off with their new houses and farms, their cash and educations. She couldn't see it.

It wasn't his job to convince her. He just had to keep her from stopping or slowing progress. So why did he feel like the job would be a failure if he didn't change her mind? He'd been in the country for such a short time, but felt he had a better grasp on what people wanted or needed than she did. She might have the heart to help, but her energies and ideas were seriously misdirected. She was looking to tomorrow. *He* was looking to fifty years from now. She was providing a fish. *He* was giving them a boat and a fishing pole.

His headlights illuminated the road just in front of him. The tall elephant grass on both sides of the road swooshed past. It gave him the sensation he was falling, falling, falling. He blinked to moisten his eyes. He glanced at the clock on the dash. It was nearly four in the morning.

He reached to turn on the radio, looking for a station to keep him awake. The search button sent the radio scanning for a station, but landed on nothing but static. He turned the radio off.

Electricity meant progress. Progress meant more good for more people. More good meant a rise in standard of living, improvements in education, better jobs. Sure, these would take time, but at least he was helping things move in the right direction. Not like Cassie, who was like some kind of outsider Luddite, trying to preserve a culture for the sake of preservation with no regard for what the actual effects of the preservation might be. She might think she was rescuing, but to him, it looked more like mummification.

His headlights flashed across something in the road. He stomped on the brake and clutched the wheel.

First the squeal of tires. Then a loud smack.

Then the bump of the front right tire and then the rear tire going up and over whatever it was.

The car swerved. The left tire caught the edge of the crumbly pavement.

The wheel wrenched out of Jason's control.

The world exploded in the cacophony of smashing glass, crunching metal. It spun over and around. Once, twice. Jason lost count of how many times he flipped.

When the car finally ground to a stop, miraculously, it was right side up. One headlight shone into the tall grass.

Jason sat completely still, taking inventory.

He seemed to have all his limbs. He tested them out. They were all functioning.

The car was a total loss. No way would he drive away from here.

Something tickled on his cheek. He put his hand up to scratch it.

He pulled his hand away and stared at it. It was covered in warm, sticky blood.

Chapter 30

JASON DIDN'T SHOW UP THE next morning.

Maybe Cassie had heard wrong. She thought he'd said he would pick her up, but maybe he'd said to meet him at the dam. She tried texting and calling, but got no response either way.

Not like she wanted to see him. She was still furious. He'd lied, cheated, and stolen her trust.

Still, if she didn't keep her promise to help clean up, a promise that hung over her, her friends would suffer for it. They were going through enough without her adding to their problems.

She checked her phone every few minutes to see if he'd texted her. Why wasn't he answering?

When Jason hadn't contacted her by midmorning, she climbed the hill herself and hired a cab to take her to the dam on the chance he'd meant for her to meet him there. He hadn't . . . but just in case. She hoped he wouldn't be there, but expected he would. She was embarrassed and riled up. She didn't want to go. But it would be far worse to not show up and jeopardize her friends' chance at freedom.

The parking lot was under water now. The taxi dropped her by the road as near the dam as it could get.

Cassie grimaced when she saw the job they'd done. Bright green paint spelled out a single word in crooked, drippy letters along the top of the dam's white face.

ME.

It couldn't be worse. It was the opposite of what she'd wanted to say. It wasn't about *me*; it was about *us*. About being in community together and fighting to preserve that community. Only she was the only one left to fight.

Below, closer to the riverbank, she spotted someone with a camera. She trudged through the grass toward him. It was Pierre. Dadgum. She'd forgotten she'd texted him to be sure he would get photos. Figured he would show up the one time she didn't want his attention.

When she got up alongside him, he asked, "How did you hear about this?"

She swallowed. "Word gets around."

At least he didn't write down her quote.

"I wonder what it means. If it is in English, it seems to be quite selfish. But if it is in Ewé, is it saying we should be in something else? That does not make sense. I cannot figure it out."

"Maybe it's not the whole message," Cassie said. "It's off center."

He looked at her, his left eyebrow raised as if he knew she knew, but he didn't challenge her.

It was supposed to say HOME, with double meaning for both languages. It was supposed to be about preserving your place in the world. But she could say none of that without admitting guilt.

"It is not personal," Pierre said. "It is progress."

"It should be," she replied. She turned away from the word. She didn't want to look at it. It was embarrassing. "When you're messing with other people's lives, it should be personal."

A group of workers walked across the top of the dam. They stopped above the giant letters. After a few minutes, a team of three was lowered over the edge. Each held a hose. A trio of pressure washers growled to life.

It didn't look like they needed her after all.

Pierre clicked another picture. He pointed his camera at her. "Hey, stand in front of the dam. I will take your picture in case you ever come up with that story."

She held her hand out. "No, thanks. I'd rather get a photo of what I stand for, not against." And she'd really like to not be remembered for her botched message.

He lowered the camera. "How is the plan for the strike coming?"

"Good," she said. "Really good." Like there was going to be a strike. "Have you seen Jason?"

"Mr. Birkman? Not today. I do not think he is here."

Why had he made her come here if he wasn't even going to be here? Just another proof of what a jerk he was. She hoped he'd leave the country and leave her alone.

"Listen," Pierre said. "If you do get that strike together, let me know. It might seem like you are not making a difference, but I admire someone who stands for something, no matter how hopeless. And I am not the only one. Just think about it."

Cassie looked at him, surprised that he seemed to want to help. "You know what? I will."

While Cassie helped Elli pack, she grieved her loss. She would miss this dear friend. They would stay friends, sure, but she knew from experience how hard it was to maintain a friendship when you lived in different towns.

All her friends were going to different towns—Elli to the new Babakondji with her parents, Benedict to the capital for university, Koffi to the cité to work as a night guard. Even Antoinette had settled on where she would go. With a fistful of cash, she planned to move back to the north and start a family with her husband. Cassie was the only one without a plan.

She wanted to beg her friends to stay, but she'd tried so many times, she knew they wouldn't listen to her. She'd botched the protest so bad, she was lucky they hadn't gone to jail.

She had left a handful of messages on Cam's Skype but hadn't heard from him since their first conversation. It was too late for him to help her hire an attorney now anyway, now that everyone had officially filed their decision with the IMAN Group. Still, when she saw she had a video message from him, she couldn't scramble up the hill fast enough to collect it.

As soon she reached two bars, she pressed play on the message, even though she wasn't in sight of the cell tower yet.

It looked like he was in his office by the dark shelving behind him. He wore a business suit with a dark red tie. He looked like such a grown-up. He leaned toward the webcam. The picture glitched out, then resolved itself again.

"Hey, Cass. Um, sorry to be slow getting back. Listen, I was hoping my company would throw some support behind you, but it didn't work out. Anyway, I have another idea that might help you. Call me."

She called, but of course he didn't answer. He was probably asleep. Calling and having someone pick up the phone simply did not happen to her.

With at least a little hope inside her, she went back down into the valley. With so much going wrong, she knew she could do one thing completely right.

She would throw the biggest party Babakondji had ever seen.

When she asked Elli if anyone would come, a smile tickled at the corner of her friend's mouth. "I think everyone would come. You will need drinks."

"And music," Cassie said. Loud music, which meant she needed to rent some speakers and an amplifier. She made a list of other things and set to work, happy to have something to keep her occupied while everyone else was preparing to leave.

Thursday night, the last one before the enforced evacuation, she dragged all her chairs out to the well. So did everyone else. Cassie set them in a huge circle around the open area. She was determined it would be an epic party, a fitting good-bye to the town and its people. She supplied soft drinks and loud music. The rest supplied itself. She'd never understand how it happened, but whenever a group was gathering—whether for a funeral or a wedding or a graduation—people came with benches, drinks, snacks for sale, and the need to dance.

It was no different tonight. People started showing up just after dark. By eight or nine, the whole town—or everyone who was still left—was there. A few of the older folks wore an air of despair, but all the young people threw off whatever misgivings they might have about leaving and fell into raucous celebration.

Cassie stood apart from the unleashed excitement, looking in on a group of people who had lived in this place, alongside each other, for generations. What would become of them now? In the morning, would they still be so happy?

For the night, she set the question aside.

A song with a loud bass line and a tempting beat blared from the speakers she'd strung from the mango tree. The partygoers melted to the edges of the yard, leaving an open area for people to dance. The teens and children took the floor first, but soon a line of older women shooed them away. Large women who spent their days tending the fire shook off the weight of their bodies and the toll of the years. Elli's mother was among them. She thrust her shoulders forward and back, rocked her elbows, stomped her feet. When all the women bent lower and lower in their dance, Cassie caught a glimpse of youth on Elli's mother's face. For her, in this moment, the worries of tomorrow didn't matter.

Cassie whooped and cheered for Ellino and the other women as they left the dance floor, making room for the old men to follow them. She laughed at the comical way the men, toothless and wiry, danced with the bravado of their younger selves.

The old men made way for the next group. Abla was the first of the young women to take center stage, but soon all the others joined her. Cassie watched, amazed, as Elli danced with pride and abandon. This was a friendship that would survive no matter what.

In the middle of the song, Elli stepped toward Cassie. She grabbed her hand and pulled her into the dance circle.

A part of Cassie resisted. She didn't have any rhythm. But tonight was not about saying no. It was about saying yes to the possibilities.

She followed Elli into the circle, to the great delight and cheers of the others. She watched Elli for cues of when to rock, when to stomp, and when to flail her elbows like chicken wings. The crowd spun around her, clapping and laughing. Laughing with her, not at her.

Tomorrow would bring its own trouble. For tonight, for this one glorious moment, she belonged.

Chapter 31

FROM HIS HOTEL ROOM, JASON got a panoramic view of the ocean. Beautiful in its shifting moods and colors, he was sick of looking at it. He'd been holed up in this room for almost a week and still wasn't cleared to leave it.

The night of the accident was blurry. He remembered flipping the car, but after that, he had some hours that were completely missing from his memory. Apparently, he had walked back to the road to look for a ride. His phone had been thrown from the car. He must have looked for it, but hadn't found it that night. Days later, Emanuel returned its mangled body to him, found by a crew the firm had hired to clean up the accident.

A Coca-Cola delivery truck picked him up and took him to the nearest hospital. He'd been transported by ambulance to a more modern facility in the capital, where he had spent a couple of days trying to convince the doctors and nurses he was fine and they should release him.

His head scan showed otherwise. They held him for observation to make sure his concussion didn't have serious side effects. When they released him, it was with the stipulation that he have round-the-clock supervision until his symptoms cleared up, which was taking much, much longer than he'd dreamed.

His head still ached most of the time and screamed in pain the rest of the time. Anywhere he had a muscle, he was sore. Simply walking across the room without falling down or throwing up was about the best he could hope for at this point.

The official cause of the accident was a herd of sheep on the road, combined with excessive speed. He was lucky it wasn't a person. There would be no charges filed.

He reached for his phone on the table beside his chair. It was identical to the old one. The IT guy at work had even been able to recover most of Jason's contacts off his SD card. The only ones missing were the ones he'd entered since arriving in Nkuve—the secretary at the project site, the chief of each of the five villages, his coworkers. Most of those, Emanuel was able to recreate for him. The one most conspicuously missing was Cassie.

He needed to call her, to explain why he hadn't shown up for her. More than that, he needed a chance to explain to her why he'd withheld who he worked for.

It shouldn't matter. Everyone from her village was already gone. In another three weeks, he would be on a plane to Nepal to help with PR on another project. This time he'd be there from the beginning. It would take longer, but it would be much easier.

It shouldn't matter, but it did.

As soon as he got medical clearance, the first thing he'd do was find Cassie and apologize.

Cassie handed a basket full of live chickens up to the taximan's assistant for him to tie atop the van. Elli and her family were already in the van, ready to move over the ridge to their new home.

The happiness and excitement of last night's party had dissipated in the reality of today.

Cassie walked to the open window nearest Elli's seat. She waved at Fabrice, Ablaga, and the others. She promised to bring them more vitamins before their supply ran out. Fabrice's hair was already growing in darker, his limbs thickening and tummy shrinking. He grinned at her and waved with two open palms.

More than anything, she wanted to beg her friend not to leave, but she wouldn't—it wouldn't be fair. A home and a future waited for her over the hilltop.

Maybe Elli really would be better off in the long run.

Cassie wanted to believe it, but she doubted it.

"Take care of my chickens," Cassie said. "Text me when you are settled in. I will come visit you."

"Are you sure you do not want them?" Elli asked. Her eyes filled with tears. "Where will you go?"

Cassie shrugged. "The chickens are yours. I don't know what I am doing yet. I know it sounds crazy, but I don't think I am finished with Babakondji."

"But the water will be here anytime."

"I know," Cassie said. "But I hear chickens don't swim well."

"What will you do next?"

"I really don't know." It had to be a grand gesture, something that sacrificed her own comfort for the sake of those she felt were being taken advantage of. She'd already ruled out a hunger strike, a protest march, and more graffiti.

"I was thinking about a sit-down strike, but there's only one of me. Besides, we already decided it was a bad idea."

"No," Elli said. "That man, the other American, was the one who said it was no good."

Jason? Was he the one who advised her against it? She couldn't recall.

Well, if he was, then it must be a great idea.

The taxi van motor started up. The assistant climbed aboard and slammed the door.

Cassie held Elli's cheek. "I will see you." She thumped the side of the van.

It pulled away.

Elli's family was the last to go. It was just Cassie and Babakondji now.

She climbed the hill one last time. Already, the edges of the new lake licked at the road leading to the village. Next time she tried to leave, she would need to go north. This way would be impassable.

Miraculously, when she dialed Cam's number, he picked up.

"Oh my lands, it's good to hear your voice."

"Yours, too." He chuckled. "You okay?"

"Yeah, yeah. Fine. It's been a crazy week, but that's all done now."

"What do you mean?"

She sighed. "I just waved the last people out of my village. They're all gone now. All but me."

"And what are your plans?"

"I'm not sure. I can't save the village, but I want to do something to keep this from happening next time they decide to build a dam. I had some ideas, but I think it's too late."

"Like what?"

She closed her eyes. Already the morning sun burned orange through her lids. "Like I don't know. Lobby to the diplomatic corps and the NGOs? I'm not very good at it, though." Considering her conversation with the ambassador, that was an understatement.

"NGOs? Okay. What else?"

"I could move to the edge of the lake and start a fish farm." She was joking. Mostly.

"Mm-hmm."

"Or . . ." Should she say it? Why not. "Or maybe do a sit-down strike in the village while it is flooding."

Silence.

"Or not," she said.

"Actually, you might be onto something there."

If she'd been chewing gum, she would have swallowed it. "Seriously?"

"Yeah. I think your only shot at making a difference is to make a big splash. This could be just what we need to get you some attention."

"What do you mean?"

"Find a place you can sit where people will find you if they come looking. Take some pictures of yourself doing your protest and send them to me. I'll see what I can do to help spread the word. We can take the 'lone voice in the wilderness' angle. People eat that kind of stuff up."

"You think?"

"I know. Trust me, Cassie. It's the way to go."

Trust me. It was their code word from way back when. It meant he was sure.

"Okay," she said. "You're the boss. A media phenomenon. That's me." If he could get the press to cover her story, she might actually be able to make a statement if not save the town.

She went back to the empty village with renewed energy. At last she had a direction now.

For a proper sit-down strike, you needed a proper chair. Her wooden armchair with no cushion was too low. She'd be drowned out in no time. She needed something with a little higher profile, something more dignified. And she knew just where to find one.

The night the chief left the village, he'd taken as much with him as he could. But he hadn't taken the elaborate carved ebony throne. This was just a ceremonial seat. The real seat of power, a simply carved low stool, was the one he chose to carry with him. The throne had the solid presence she required, and would offer gravitas to what she knew would be a ridiculous feat.

She let herself into the chief's compound. The chair still sat in the place where he used to hold court before he'd sold out his village. Its high back, carved with primitive images of the African beasts so conspicuously missing from this land, stretched as tall as her head. She grabbed both arms and lifted.

The chair didn't budge.

Puzzled, she looked around the back and feet to see if it was anchored in place. She didn't see anything indicating it was. She bent her knees and tried lifting it again.

It barely wiggled.

No wonder the chief had left it here. This thing weighed a ton.

She stood back and looked at it. There must be a way to move it. She walked behind it and pulled as hard as she could on the back. It tipped toward her just a little before thwumping back to the ground.

She should probably choose a different chair, but now that she had this one on her mind, she wouldn't be satisfied with any other. No way was this monster going to float. As the symbol of the chief's family, the chief who was the first to abandon ship, it made poetic sense to her that it also be the symbol of the one who stayed.

She needed a way to move the blasted thing, though, or the whole idea about getting publicity would be hidden behind compound walls. She needed to get this chair out in the open for the whole world to see.

She would move this thing, even if she had to do it an inch at a time.

She found a kekevi. The hand-hewn wooden cart didn't look strong enough to carry more than a few pounds, much less the chair, but people had been making and using them for all sorts of hauling for generations. She sat on it to test its strength and pushed herself down the path a few yards with her feet. Its slats dug into her rump. It might resemble a wagon, but it was definitely not designed for comfort. The wheels were all different sizes, so it wobbled as it rolled, but it seemed strong enough for the job.

She grabbed the braided rope handle and dragged the kekevi to the chief's house. A couple of loose bricks from the yard could serve as chocks. There wasn't enough room behind the chair to back the wagon up to it, so she parked alongside it.

She grabbed the chair and pulled as hard as she could. It didn't move.

Shoot.

Around the other side, she dug her feet into the ground, put her back against the arm of the chair, and pushed. It tipped a little. She ground her feet in and pushed harder. It made no difference. She relaxed and let the chair settle to the ground with a thunk.

How in the world was she supposed to move this chair to where she needed it?

She tried dragging it with a rope.

She walked through the village more than once, yelling in case someone happened to have stayed behind. No one answered. She was truly alone here. That was a first.

She sat in the chair right where it was and wished it was a good enough spot. But it wasn't.

Finally, with the combined power of a long lever, a good pry point, and a lot of loud grunting, she managed to tip the chair onto the kekevi. Dragging it to the open space near the well went a little easier—a little, but not much— and tipping it back up was like standing up a sleeping elephant.

She stood it in place under the gourd tree. She was farther from the trunk than she'd intended, but at this point, she was calling it perfect. Here by the main entrance to Babakondji, any reporter who came to town was sure to find her with no trouble. If they didn't mind wading once the crick started to rise.

She texted Pierre, excited to finally have a strike he could cover. If things went as planned, by noon tomorrow, every paper in the region—maybe even the television crew—would be reporting on the one person who stood against the damage done by the world's newest lake.

Chapter 32

THE NEXT MORNING, CASSIE planted herself in the ebony chair at the base of the gourd tree. She'd always liked the tree, with its dozens of watermelon-sized gourds dangling from low, twisted branches. It belonged in a quirky kids' movie. She'd chosen it as the tree she would sit under because of its irony. The very tree that supplied Babakondji with vessels for fetching water would be her shelter while she waited for the water she wouldn't have to fetch.

It was late morning before she noticed the ground beneath her was growing soft. The water level underground must be rising. So many plants, thirsty for rain, would revive at the first taste of fresh water, only to be smothered by the excess of the very thing they craved.

The reporters could show up anytime. True, the saturation didn't look too dramatic, but it was something.

It took most of the day for the water to soak the ground. At this rate, she'd be sitting here for a very long time. She snapped a selfie with the gourd tree in the background.

She was surprised no reporters had come today. They were probably waiting for the waters to rise a little more. That's all right. She could wait.

She texted Cam to see if her photos had gone through, but she didn't hear back from him.

Since no one was here, she might as well go home and get some sleep. Her apartment floor was nearly a foot above ground level. Her bed sat several inches above that. It was silly of her to sit in protest when there wasn't even anyone around to see her. She might as well make use of the perfectly good bed she had at home.

She'd get a good night's rest and continue her protest in the morning. The reporters would come tomorrow. Or maybe the next day.

When they did, she would be waiting.

As dramatic protests went, this one was falling flat. She expected the water to rise quicker once it penetrated the ground, but it was barely deeper in the morning than the night before. She went back out to her chair to wait for the news crews to arrive.

After a few minutes, she sloshed back home and grabbed her well-worn copy of *The Hunger Games* to read while she waited for the media. She texted Pierre to remind him of her strike, then opened to chapter 1 and began to read.

By the time Katniss risked her life to get Peeta the medicine he needed, the sun rode high in the sky.

Cassie looked down. The water had crept an inch or two up the legs of her chair. The air hung thick enough to squeeze. If she reached out, she could grasp fistfuls of it and press raindrops out. Her skin prickled. The water pooling beneath her chair looked so refreshing. She shouldn't, especially since she sat in protest against it, but she wanted nothing more than to splash her feet into the gathering water.

She looked around to make sure no one was there before lowering her feet. Tepid. Disappointed, she pulled her feet back up, moisture hanging on them like sweat, refusing to evaporate into the already saturated air.

The sun hung motionless, stuck in its slide across the sky. She mopped her face with her shirtsleeve.

She tried to get back into her book, but it was too hot to read. She wondered what her friends were up to. Had Elli settled in her new house? Did she like it? What about Koffi? Was he good at his job? And Benedict, who had taken the money so he could pay for university—would he even pass the entrance exams? If they got everything they'd agreed on, was there even a reason for her to strike? How long should she give the reporters before she gave up?

She mopped her forehead again and again. In the late afternoon, she waded away from her chair so she could take a picture of it. She texted the picture to Cam and Pierre.

Cam wrote back immediately.

It is rising! You're doing great! Keep the pics coming. Don't give up!

It didn't feel like she was accomplishing anything, but if Cam thought they would come, she would stay. She wished she could get Internet down here. She felt stranded without being able to make phone calls.

When the sun moved far enough that the gourd tree no longer offered shade, Cassie unwrapped the avo from around her waist. She stood on the chair and arranged the cloth in the branches in a way that would keep her out of direct sunlight.

She finished her book as evening fell. The water had risen to just under the seat of her chair. By morning, she might have to climb the tree. For tonight, though, she waded back to her house. No use losing sleep if no one was there to see her objections. How did Gandhi stick with his protests? And how did his refusal to eat while in the privacy of his own home translate to an entire nation rallying behind his cause?

Maybe her cause wasn't big enough, important enough.

If an aid worker drowned in a dying village, did she ever really exist?

And if the company she was fighting didn't know it was in a battle, could there ever be a winner?

The next day she took up her spot again, but with even less enthusiasm than before. During the night, the water had finally breached the threshold of her apartment. She could have sandbagged it to keep water from pouring in under her door, but it wouldn't have helped for long. She'd already noticed water seeping in through cracks in the walls. The old rental was as watertight as a colander.

The seat of her chair was covered. Barely, but enough.

One of the plastic chairs she originally thought of using floated nearby.

She stood on the seat of the ebony throne, grabbed hold of a limb, and swung herself up into the first layer of the gourd tree's branches. This was seriously the lamest sit-down strike in history. Gandhi went on a hunger strike and freed his people. Martin Luther King drummed up a million men and changed the landscape of a nation. She sat in a tree and got a splinter, and there was no one to see it or to offer her tweezers.

The world was strangely silent. There should be children playing, women chattering at the nearby well, chickens clucking out a mournful song. Now it was just her in a tree surrounded by a two-foot-deep lake.

Cassie repositioned herself to get more comfortable. She closed her eyes and listened to the gentle lapping of water against the trunk of her tree. She wouldn't be going back to her bed tonight. How long would she last in this tree if no one came to take her picture? There was no point to a protest if the ones you were fighting didn't even know you existed.

The light dimmed, then brightened again. She opened her eyes and looked around. Giant clouds gathered to the west. Those would definitely dump a storm wherever they passed. Babakondji had not had its first rain of the season yet. Any other year, she'd be praying for rain to fall on the fields of her neighbors. Today, the fields were gone. They didn't need the rain anyway. And she certainly didn't need it either. Today, she prayed for the rain to pass her by and fall on someone who wanted it.

The clouds darkened and tumbled toward her. The air turned a sickening green. The sky grumbled and growled, rolling thunder back and forth.

Cassie watched, transfixed by the power and beauty.

A flash of lightning crackled across the sky overhead, followed immediately by a deafening boom.

What was she doing sitting in a tree? She needed to find shelter. She didn't love the idea of wading through thigh-deep water either. Which was worse?

She didn't know.

The sky opened and dumped bathtubs of rain. Another flash of lightning. Another crack and boom, even louder.

The tree was worse.

Cassie scrambled off her branch and landed in the water with a splash. Her knees buckled, sending her face-first into the water. She jumped up and looked around for the closest safe place. Better to head for shore and look for high ground. The water pulled her back, but she fought forward.

Hair hung in her eyes. She pushed it aside, but still couldn't see for all the rain falling in her face. One foot in front of the other.

The sky lit again.

She held her breath.

The thunder cracked a second later. Was it moving away?

She couldn't take her chances. She kept moving as fast as she could.

Just beyond the edge of the water, she took shelter under the bicycle repairman's agbado. The thatched shelter offered protection from the rain falling straight down, but was no help against the rain blowing sideways in the thrashing wind. Vaguely, through the downpour, she could see the gourd tree being pummeled. She was glad she hadn't tried to ride out the storm.

A text chimed in from Pierre.

Are you still on strike?

She answered him.

Yes. Where are you?

On assignment. I will see if they can send one of our floaters to interview you. No promises.

When the rain passed, she waded with renewed resolve back to the tree through water that was a little deeper than before the storm. It might be stupid, but she had to see this through. Even without the media, she couldn't quit. But she sure did hope a reporter would come soon. She felt silly out here all by herself.

She thought of all the abandoned projects in her yard—the baskets, the muffins, the chicken tractor. This time she would not give up. No matter what.

Chapter 33

SHE GOT LITTLE SLEEP THAT night. Despite pulling her pillow into the tree and wrapping herself in an avo to protect herself from mosquitoes, she could not get comfortable. Every time she closed her eyes, she felt like she was falling. She jerked awake. She was still secure on her branch.

She took her second avo and used it to tie herself to the limb. At least that way if she slipped, she wouldn't land in the drink.

Sometime before the early morning light, she drifted off again.

She awakened to the sound of splashing.

She opened her eyes, hoping to see one of Pierre's floaters splashing out for an interview.

It was Jason. Jason, who she hadn't seen since the night she'd painted the dam.

He sat below her in an aluminum canoe. She hadn't seen one of those since she left the States.

Jason, who she had hoped to never see again.

Jason, who had a gauze bandage plastered on his forehead. What had happened to him?

He splashed water up at her with the tip of his paddle. "Morning, Glory."

If she had been in a bed, she would have turned over and pulled the covers over her head. She shot him a dirty look. With as much bile as she could muster, she spit, "What are you doing here?"

"I came to see the stubbornest person in the world. Have you seen her?"

"I think it's a *he*. Go away." She switched positions so he couldn't look at her face.

He paddled around to see her face. Below his bandage he sported an impressive black eye. Something bad had happened that kept him from picking her up last Friday. He'd been hurt. Well, she wouldn't give him the satisfaction of asking what happened. He seemed fine now. She wouldn't mention it.

She wondered if he was in a lot of pain. She shook it off. It was none of her business.

Jason said, "Come down. I need to apologize."

"What for?"

"Do I have to do it while you're up a tree?"

"Yes."

"Okay, then. I'm sorry. I didn't mean to lie to you. I mean, at first, I thought it was better if you didn't know who I worked for. But then my company was the enemy, and I didn't know how to tell you I worked for them. I was afraid it would drive you away. And I didn't want that."

No wonder they paid him the big bucks for negotiations. He sounded so sincere.

"Come on, Cassie. Why don't you come down?"

She turned away from him and crossed her arms. "I'm waiting for someone."

"Who?" He spread his arms out. "You've been out here for days. If they were going to come, they would have come."

"They're coming. Pierre said. If there was a protest, he would come. That's what he said."

"Why isn't he here, then?"

"He is sending someone."

"How many days has it been?"

He knew as well as she did. Three days, and Jason was the one who had to show up? Why not Pierre? Or Elli or one of her friends? Or anyone else? She thought she was fighting with them, or at least for them. Now it seemed she was just fighting near them.

Still, she would not give Jason the satisfaction of seeing her quit. If she was coming down, it would be on her own terms, in her own time, and when he wasn't watching.

"You know the flooding is almost done, don't you?"

She looked down at him. "What do you mean?"

"This is as deep as it's going to get. Are you going to sit in that tree forever in protest of something that's already done?"

"Wait, what?" She must have heard wrong. "It's only two feet deep."

"Yeah, that's the plan."

"Y'all ruined my home for two feet of water?"

"Do you think anyone would want to live here now? We had to evacuate."

"You could have filled the reservoir a little less. Or moved the village like fifty feet. You didn't have to send everyone away."

Two feet of water? She couldn't believe that's what she'd been fighting all this time.

Jason rowed his canoe over to the plastic chair that was still floating near the ebony one. He grabbed it with one hand and, with the other, used his oar to paddle to the shore near the agbado where Cassie had waited out the storm. He jumped out of the canoe and pulled it onto dry land. He sat down on the plastic chair.

"What are you doing?" she called.

"Waiting for you to come down and talk some sense."

"I'm not coming down."

"That's all right. I can wait."

He took out his phone and snapped a picture of her.

"What are you doing?" He'd probably pass it around the office so they could all mock her.

"I'm setting it as my wallpaper. Someday we're going to laugh about this, you know."

"I won't," she said.

"Sure you will." He snapped another picture. "Trust me."

Cassie didn't figure bathroom breaks into this ridiculous strike. Nor did she figure that her mortal enemy would be staring at her the whole time, daring her to give up.

By about four in the afternoon, she didn't care about any of that. All she could think about was how bad she needed to go.

She crossed her legs and tried not to think about the lake below her.

Water, water, everywhere, and all boards did shrink.

The peaceful lapping of water moving against the trunk of her tree mocked her. She crossed her legs the other way and squeezed her muscles.

Water, water, everywhere, nor any drop to drink.

She found herself very thirsty. The last thing she needed was to feed her bladder more liquid. She swallowed some spit.

She looked across at Jason.

He smiled and waved at her.

How did that magician who stood on the column in New York City not go to the bathroom? For that matter, what about those saints who spent years and years on top of a pillar? They must have had a support staff. Or scheduled potty breaks.

Her bladder screamed. Could it explode if you held it too long? Could you poison your blood by not peeing?

She tried thinking about something else . . . anything else. She wanted to solve the problem of the dam and this stupid situation she'd put herself in, but she couldn't concentrate. At all.

She counted to a thousand, then started over again. She picked at the tree bark next to her, slowly carving her initials out with her fingernails. A sliver pierced under her nail.

"Ow!" she cried.

"You okay?" Jason called.

"Oh, you're still here?" Like she didn't know. "I'm fine." She sucked on her finger, hoping to soften and loosen the sliver. It hurt like crazy. She tasted blood. When she pulled her finger away, the sliver was still there, embedded in a stripe of red under her nail. She rifled in her bag for a pocketknife. Her hand shook with the effort of staying in the tree, worrying about cutting her finger, and the constant pain of needing a bathroom.

After several tries, she finally caught the end of the sliver with the tip of her knife. With a gentle pull, it came free.

She sucked her finger until the bleeding stopped.

At least she'd solved one thing today. She looked across the water.

Jason still stared at her.

Finally . . . finally, the sun touched the horizon. It wouldn't be long now. Dusk to dark took no time at all this close to the equator. She could hold it. She had to.

At last the sky darkened enough that she couldn't see Jason anymore. Soon her eyes would adjust to the starlight. This was the moment.

She lowered herself carefully out of the tree. She dropped the last few feet into the water, squatted just low enough, and felt enormous relief. She'd never felt so good in her life.

Suddenly, a bright light shone in her face.

She threw her hand up to block the light from blinding her. It was coming from Jason's direction.

"You giving up?" he asked.

"No," she stammered. "I—I just slipped is all. I'm fine. Turn that off."

Embarrassed, she climbed back into the tree, the last place she wanted to be right now. She wished he would just go away and leave her alone. Her wet shorts stuck to her legs. The heat would not dissipate for hours yet. Her clothes clung to her, sweat mixed with water. She could really use a shower.

Ha! That was an understatement. Now she couldn't think about anything besides what a long, cool shower might feel like. Her last real shower was a hundred years ago when she'd gone to the embassy party to ask for help with her microloan project for her friends. Since then, she'd only bathed with a bucket of water in the space behind her house.

"Hey, Cassie?" Jason's voice came to her through the dark.

"What do you want?"

"You don't have to do this, you know. You could go to a hotel for the night and come back to your tree in the morning."

"As if. I'm not coming down."

"Just for the night. It'd be more comfortable."

Well, that would defeat the whole purpose. Though, with the thought of a nice bed and a real shower, it was kind of hard to remember what the purpose was anyway. Who was she protesting for? What was she striking against? The people she was for were gone; the thing she was against was already in place.

But she'd promised herself she wouldn't quit until someone heard her lone voice.

"No one will know," he said.

He would know.

"I will know," she said. Her words sank in. It hit her that this protest wasn't about the dam anymore. It wasn't about her friends and neighbors. It was about her. She'd always been good at coming up with big ideas and plans, but she rarely followed them through to success. Well, this time she wasn't giving up. She whispered, "I will know."

Jason's headlamp came on again, a bright spot of light against the darkness. It swung back and forth, finally landing on the canoe. He pulled something from the bottom of the boat with both hands. Whatever it was, it was big. It made a long sweeping sound as he pulled it toward the bow. He lifted it, his light dimming behind whatever it was that blocked him from sight, then brightening again as he unfurled a hammock with an attached mosquito net.

He tied the hammock to two posts of the agbado and climbed in. He clicked off his headlamp, dunking the world in darkness again.

Cassie leaned back on her branch and waited for her eyes to adjust. One by one, the stars came into focus. Down near the horizon, the stars were shrouded by heavy humidity, but overhead, they shone bright and clear. She easily found the Southern Cross on one end of the sky and the North Star on the other. The lynx, the lion, and the centaur marched along the path between them. Those tiny pinpricks of light moved in their path, night after night, as they had since creation. Her own troubles paled in comparison. What was it they said? Life is a mist? She'd never felt it more than she did tonight. She'd done what she could, but it was time to move on. But move on to what? If she climbed out of this tree without a plan, she'd lose more than her home. She'd lose face with Jason and with her friends. Even more than that, she'd lose her self-respect.

Her hopes and dreams for Babakondji were not wrong. It was good to help people better their circumstances. It was good to teach them life skills to help them survive in a changing world. But now, with Babakondji under water, she needed to think bigger. How could she help the people of a village that didn't exist anymore?

A rooster crowed.

Cassie checked her phone. Four in the morning. Where the myth that roosters crowed at dawn came from, she didn't know. Nkuve roosters crowed whenever they pleased.

She shone her light toward the water's edge, looking for the offending rooster. He perched in the crook of a tree, proud of his dominion.

"Go to sleep," Cassie whispered to the rooster.

"I'm trying," Jason whispered back. "But this stupid bird won't let me. I'm thinking about fried chicken for breakfast."

She couldn't help smiling. That was one old rooster. After years of free-range foraging, he'd be tougher'n leather. "I'd rather eat bushrat." Or gruel or almost anything. She was getting hungry.

"I remember," Jason said, his voice barely above a whisper.

Chapter 34

CASSIE SNUCK OUT OF THE TREE before dawn so she didn't have a repeat of last night's painful episode. Before climbing back into the tree, she stood on the ebony chair, wrapped herself in a clean avo, and quickly changed her shorts and undergarments beneath it. Moments like this made her realize how far she'd come since the days she wouldn't change clothes in front of the other girls in her cabin at camp. Africa had a way of bringing out the common humanity in everyone, even her.

She checked her phone to see if she'd had any new messages from Cam or Pierre, but her phone was dead. The car battery was probably drowned by now.

At first light, Jason lit a fire. The smell of freshly brewed coffee reached her in her perch. If that wasn't enough, the sound and smell of sizzling bacon wafted her way.

"Now, that's not fair!" she said. "World wars have been won with the smell of bacon."

He grinned at her and held up the pan in her direction. "Want some?"

Boy, did she.

But first things had to come first.

"Hey, Jason?" How was she going to ask this?

"Yeah?"

"I have an idea."

"What's that?" He walked to the water's edge and made eye contact.

She had his attention now.

"I've had some time for thinking."

"And?"

"And I'm pretty good at what I do. I have a big heart and I like helping people."

"Me, too, Cassie. We just have different ideas of what is the best kind of help."

She swallowed. Here's where she needed to keep her pride from popping out. She swallowed again. "I know you're not destroying people's lives on purpose."

He crossed his arms. "I'm not destroying people's lives at all. People who refuse to bend are bound to snap. But for those who are willing to change with progress, we're offering a step up."

She shook her head. "I know you believe that, but you don't see what happens to those people after you leave."

"Like what?"

"Like Ngorogo."

"That wasn't our project."

"It doesn't matter who did the PR or the HR or any of that. It's disgraceful how those people have been treated. All the promises, all the same ones you're making here, were empty. They are living in crumbling houses. They never got their money. Their land is unfarmable. I don't want the same thing to happen to my people."

"It won't."

"How do you know that? What's to keep it from happening?" She heard her voice rise.

Stay calm. Don't panic. Build your case.

She took a deep breath.

"I—it won't happen here. I'll make sure of it."

"And how are you going to do that? Are you staying?"

"Me? No. I'm moving on, but I can keep communication open with Emanuel. And I always return to former projects to make sure the plans stay on track."

Cassie shook her head. "Emanuel is too far removed from his village roots. He looks down on people like they're worth less because they have less."

"If not him, then who?"

Cassie leaned forward on her branch, hugging the limb in front of her for support. Now or never.

"Me."

"What?"

She cleared her throat and spoke louder, with what she hoped sounded like more confidence. "Me. I'm the right man for the job. I love these people. I know them. And I'm not afraid to do whatever it takes to make sure they get what they deserve."

"I'll say." Jason stepped back to the fire and flipped the bacon over, strip by strip.

Cassie didn't know her mouth could water so much and be so dry at the same time. She waited for a response.

Jason stood up. He walked behind the agbado, then out of sight. Surely he wasn't leaving? Not with bacon on the fire. Not with her hanging in this tree. Not with her white flag waving in the wind.

Shoot.

She waited for him to come back. And waited. And waited.

Even without him, she'd done what she could. She knew she couldn't help her friends by trying to be exactly like them. She was unique, and it was the things that made her herself that might bring real value, not only to the people of Babakondji, but to Ngorogo and other places as well.

Besides, she couldn't let the bacon burn.

She lowered her feet to the chair and stood on it. She stepped one foot, then the other into the water and waded to shore.

She didn't need Jason or anyone else to help her be heard. She just needed to be true to her own voice. And that meant being American. In Africa. She didn't have to become a local to help the locals. She couldn't become a local really. Not here. She could only do that if she moved back to Arkansas, which she wasn't ready to do.

Just as she reached dry land, Jason stepped into sight from behind a couple of palm nut trees.

Cassie stopped. She looked back at the gourd tree. To be true to her strike, she really should take her perch again. She sure didn't want to. She wanted breakfast. She looked to Jason and then back at the tree. She took a couple of reluctant steps into the water.

"Wait. Where are you going?"

She hesitated.

He stepped to the edge of the lake and reached for her hand. He led her onto dry land. "Yes," he said.

"Yes what?"

"Yes, I have a response. And yes. You're hired. It's a great idea. Who is going to follow through better than you?

Who else could make sure people get what they need and deserve, what they've been promised?"

"What *you* promised," she said.

"Right. What I promised, but what the power company promised, too. You'll work for my company, but ETN will also work with you directly. You develop a plan—both for here and up north—and we'll make it happen. Are you interested?"

Interested? She was ecstatic. "I—how—it's—" She couldn't seem to choke out a coherent thought. It had happened so fast. It was exactly what she wanted. She finally pulled together a thought and blurted out, "Yes!"

He reached for her hand and led her out of the water.

She smelled terrible. She was filthy.

She had never been so happy in her life.

She gently touched his bandage. "What happened?"

"Driving after dark. I hit a sheep. Apparently it isn't safe to drive at night here. Wish someone had told me." He winked, then winced.

"Ouch," she said.

He motioned for her to take a seat by the fire. He pulled the pan of bacon off the heat and set it aside.

She shook her head. "I can't believe you're the one who came. I waited so long."

"Who did you expect?"

"I was hoping for Pierre or anyone else from the media. All this time and no one even knows I am here."

He held her at arm's length. "What are you talking about?"

She shrugged. "I was trying to get someone's attention, make a statement to the press, to the world, but it didn't work. Just like every other project I've tried."

He laughed. "You don't know?"

"Know what?"

He laughed again. "You really don't know. I can't believe it. Cassie Perth, everyone knows."

"What do you mean?"

"You are all over the Internet. Every social media site, every media outlet. You're everywhere. The voice of the voiceless. Look." He held out his phone.

She grabbed it. Was he serious?

It didn't take long to see he was completely serious. He had preloaded a bunch of sites. Her close-up was everywhere, the one of her in the tree with water below.

She *had* been heard. Her throat tightened. Tears of joy pooled and threatened to fall. She didn't want to cry. "Thank you," she whispered, though she didn't know what she was thanking him for exactly. For being there. For showing her.

Her stomach growled.

Jason grinned. "I see how it's gonna be. You only like me for my bacon."

She grinned. "Well, it's not the *only* reason, but it's up there."

Chapter 35

CASSIE GLANCED AT THE CLOCK. She had enough time to make a couple more calls before meeting Jason for the dedication.

She spun all the way around in her office chair. She still couldn't believe the ETN had set her up with such a nice office. The air-conditioning alone had changed her life. But she wasn't closed up in here. It was just a place to regroup between her favorite parts of the job, being in the villages helping people.

Her people.

She tapped "A" on her phone's keypad and selected "Andy" from the pick list.

Hi, Andy. My name's Cassie. SJ gave me your number. I'm lining up folks to help make things right in the flooded villages. Can I call you about it sometime?

The answer came back right away.

Sure. Let's talk.

They exchanged a few more notes to set up an in-person meeting. She had a good feeling about this guy being able to offer some real help to the people of the northern and central Bodo regions.

She looked at the clock again. She didn't want to be late.

She checked to make sure her topknot was secure and her new linen dress wasn't too, too wrinkled. So much had changed in two short weeks. She felt like an adult with a grown-up job.

With her purse hooked on one arm and keys in the other hand, she whisked out the door into the blistering sun. Within seconds, her dress wilted and her loose wisps of hair stuck to the skin on her neck and cheeks.

Some things never changed.

Cassie looked at her keychain and found the little button with the open lock. She pressed it twice. A horn beeped.

Her horn. She climbed into the driver's seat of the Hilux pickup, still in shock that it was hers as a tool of the job. Speaking of tools, she needed to pick up Niko and his load of fishnets. She swung by the net factory on her way to the dam.

With her truck bed filled with neatly folded nets and Niko in the passenger's seat beside her, she didn't feel quite as guilty about driving in an air-conditioned vehicle.

Niko looked like he was in heaven.

Jason and Cam both said she shouldn't feel guilty at all, that she needed the truck to get around to all her villages, but all the opulence was overwhelming.

Speaking of overwhelming, she was still floored by how much attention she'd received on social media. While she thought she was sitting alone in the middle of a slowly forming lake, she was actually trending on Twitter, on Facebook, on Instagram and Snapchat, and a bunch of other places including something called Vine that she'd never heard of. Now that she was working with the ETN, she would be able to leverage the fame to call in favors from the States.

She approached the dam from the south. Its broad white face showed only the faintest evidence of her botched vandalism career. You couldn't even make out the word, thank goodness. She pulled under a tent stretched across the road. A valet took her keys and drove off with her pickup and her instructions to keep an eye on the fishing nets in the back. She hadn't had time to purchase a canopy yet, so anything in the bed of the truck was vulnerable, though she suspected security today to be high. Niko wasn't attending the ceremony, but he couldn't be expected to sit in a hot car. He said he wanted to visit a friend in the area and that he'd meet her later. She wished she could invite him as her plus one, but she was learning not to ask for too much too fast.

Another large tent stood near the top of the dam, shading a podium and rows of plastic chairs. Most of the guests gathered under or near the tent, shade seekers all.

The sun burned white overhead. Even though she wasn't facing it, she squinted in the brightness. With her hand shading her eyes, she looked to see if she recognized anyone. The first one to catch her eye was Chief Gbeze. There were a few things about this new job she wouldn't enjoy. Building a working relationship with her former chief was one of them.

"Cassandra!" he called, waving her over with a grin. He apparently didn't share her misgivings.

She made her way over to him, pasting on a smile she hoped masked her lack of enthusiasm. Nearby, she spotted the ambassador and her husband chatting with the head of the ETN. She reached out her hand. "Chief. It's been a long time."

"Too long. How are you?"

"Oh, fine. You heard I've moved to the capital? But I'll be back on a regular basis."

He nodded. "You will do a good job. I know you care about my people."

From him, it was high praise. It didn't exactly make her like him, but it made her hate him a little less.

A hand on her elbow interrupted their conversation. She turned to see Jason, freshly pressed as usual. She had no idea how he did that. Besides the hint of bruising under his eye, you would never know he'd almost been killed in an accident. "Hi!" She gripped his hand and squeezed it, and shot him a look she hoped would say, "Get me out of here."

He spoke to the chief. "Sorry I need to steal her away, but I need to speak with Miss Perth for a moment."

"Of course, Mr. Birkman."

It hadn't even occurred to her until this second that these two knew each other, that Jason had been the one to arrange the chief's job with the dam. It was probably the first thing he'd done when he arrived in Nkuve. Before, she would have hated him for it. Now, she reminded herself they were both working for the good of others. They just had different ideas about it.

Jason whispered to her, "We've only got a few minutes before the dedication ceremony starts. There's someone I want you to meet."

He led her toward a man whose back was to them. He had broad shoulders and wore an olive-green jacket and pants. When he turned around, Cassie recognized him. It was the president of Nkuve.

The last time she'd stood face to face with someone in power, it hadn't gone well at all, and that was just an ambassador. This was a president.

He clicked his heels together once and bowed slightly in her direction.

"Sir," she said. "Cassandra Perth. It is an honor to meet you."

He clasped her hand between both of his. "I know who you are, Miss Perth. You are the one who speaks for the people. I want to thank you for not giving up. Your strange protest brought great attention to our small nation."

Her jaw fell open.

He knew who she was. *He* wanted to thank *her*.

Jason gently tapped her elbow again.

Cassie closed her mouth. "Thank you, sir. It was my pleasure."

After another pleasantry or two, Jason and Cassie moved away from the president in search of their seats. They chose two seats together in the section reserved for ETN and IMAN representatives. Cassie hardly felt she belonged.

The head of the power company greeted them from the podium, encouraging everyone to find their chairs so the dedication could begin. While he made a long and pompous speech about the benefits this project would bring to the country of Nkuve, Cassie thought about the good that had been done by the man sitting next to her. Despite everything, she was glad he'd come.

In a few short weeks in the country, Jason had moved Elli and her family from a mud house to a cement one. He had provided Niko with a lake in which to start a fishing business. He had helped Koffi line up a regular job. He had negotiated a high enough compensation for Benedict that he could fulfill his lifelong dream of attending university. That alone would change the future of his family line.

She still had her doubts that the houses would stand, that the jobs would last, that the farms would produce, but now she had a seat at the table of people who could actually do something to make sure all those things and more would happen if they could get their fingers unstuck from all the red tape. That's what she was here for.

When the ceremony had ended, when the toasts had all been proposed, the speeches all spoken, Cassie went to get her car.

A child dressed in his khaki school uniform stood on the other side of the road, behind an invisible line that separated him from the festivities.

Cassie waved at him and smiled. "Good evening," she called.

"Good evening," he called back. He gave her a thumbs-up signal. "Good evening, Cass-ahn-drah."

Not *yovo*. Not *white woman*. Not even *Mama* or *Auntie*.

A warm glow filled her. Not a hot and sweaty warmth, but a comforting, happy one.

He knew her name.

Acknowledgments

A special piece of my heart belongs to the courageous women of Togo, West Africa. While this is a fictional story set in a fictional country, I draw so much experience and wisdom from women like Lydia, Suzanne, Dela, Ajo, Ablavino, Blandine, and so many others. I couldn't have written *Saving Sorrow* without them.

Thank you to my writing group that meets at Barnes & Noble for reading chapters as I finished them and to Amy and Lori for their feedback and their honest insights. Special thanks to Nathan for the title. In my experience, those are the hardest words of the book to write.

Thanks to Jessica for the cover design, Johnathan for capturing the cover image, and Carolyn for her superior editorial eye.

Thanks to all who read my first book and asked me when I would write another. Your encouragement spurs me on.

And especially, I thank God, who writes his stories of hope and home in the hearts of his people.

About the Author

PATTY SLACK SPENT SEVEN YEARS IN WEST AFRICA.

She relates in this story to Cassie's sense of belonging. Patty's Ewé-speaking side, named Venavino, is at home in the marketplaces and courtyards of Africa.

Saving Sorrow is the first of what she hopes will be many novels set in West Africa. Sign up to receive news about upcoming releases at pattyslack.com. Patty's first novel, *Closing the Gap*, released in 2014.

Patty, her husband, and their three daughters make their home in the Northwest.

To receive occasional updates on Patty Slack's fiction, sign up for her email newsletter at pattyslack.com

26461276R00169

Made in the USA
San Bernardino, CA
30 November 2015